Ellen Baxter

FALLEN ANGEL

*

WHAT WAS THAT NOISE?

AUSTIN MACAULEY™
PUBLISHERS LTD.

A CIP catalogue record for this title is available from the British Library.

ISBN 9781786934819 (Paperback)
ISBN 9781786934826 (E-Book)
www.austinmacauley.com

First Published (2017)
Austin Macauley Publishers Ltd.™
25 Canada Square
Canary Wharf
London
E14 5LQ

Dedication

I would like to dedicate this book to my friend and former English tutor, Rachel Kearton: without her encouragement I am not sure I would have started this journey.

You have been my inspiration and for that I thank you wholeheartedly.

FALLEN ANGEL

Introduction

It was 1961, a cold wintery morning in the East End, a lone figure dressed in not much more than cheap rags was briskly walking albeit in the shadows as if hiding from the beginnings of the daily hustle and bustle of a typical East End market day. As the figure passed under a street light still lit as the morning light struggled to penetrate the fog it was in fact a woman clutching a bundle tightly to her bosom, she peered around her, furtively searching for a familiar face, seeing none she hurried along her way. No one really paid attention to anyone, everyone was out for a purpose, starting the early morning shift, setting up a market stall, deliveries to local shops everyone oblivious to the others around.

The East End was on the whole a rough part of London but filled with a wide mixture of people, Irish, African, Indian, Spanish and many more but the camaraderie was good, people looked out for each other and nobody's business was private someone always knew someone who knew someone! This was both good and bad in many ways, the gangs ran the streets and everyone knew where they stood, friendships and loyalties ran deep.

As the lone woman rounded the corner she slowed, careful not to slip on the wet pavement, the Memorial

Hospital was within sight, its night lights still burning bright in the bleakness of the early hour, a cold start to another day. She slowly mounted the steps, paused and looked around her, she then carried on through the door that led into the warmth of a reception area which was empty, she bent down and laid the bundle on a chair, with tears streaming down her face she whispered, "I'm sorry, my love, please forgive me." She glanced around her again and crept back out into the cold of the morning.

Chapter 1

Eliza Fenwick was born into this world in the early hours of a September morning; she was the much-wanted daughter of William and Briony. Both were in their early forties and had all but given up hope of ever being blessed with a child. Briony had always been a little delicate, susceptible to the slightest colds and infections; she had been a very sickly child. Over the years she had never been able to carry a child for much more than four or five months, she had miscarried seven times and the pain had worsened each time so that in the end they had both decided that enough was enough and they stopped trying, resigning themselves to a life without children. However now all that seemed a lifetime away as she lay there holding her healthy baby daughter in her arms. This small, perfect little girl had made her life and her heart complete, William sat next to her equally enthralled with this tiny person that they had made, he raised his eyes and looked lovingly at his wife whom he still loved as much today as he had when she walked down the aisle to him, the most beautiful bride fit for a king. September 7th 1944 was now the second happiest day of his life, "Briony," he whispered. She looked across to him with eyes that shone with pure love and joy, "I love you and thank you for giving me such a beautiful daughter."

Briony smiled and reached for him; kissing him with a fervent passion she had and still felt for this handsome man who was her husband. The moment was interrupted by a light tap on the door; the nurse poked her head around the door and asked if all was well to which Briony replied, "All is more than well; all is perfect!"

The nurse came over to the bed and looked down at the pink swathed bundle at the content little girl she had helped deliver a couple of hours ago. She had delivered hundreds of babies in her time and each one was as special as the one before, each held a small place in her heart "Well I'll be off away to my home now then and I'll see you tonight when I'm back on."

"Thank you for everything," Briony responded, blushing.

The nurse tutted and with a big smile she gently scolded her, "Ah be away with you woman!" With that she turned on her heel and was gone.

Chapter 2

Della Jenkins loved her job, she had helped more women than she'd had hot dinners and was thrilled every time a birth went well, of course it wasn't always a happy ending and for a moment Della paused in thought, then as quickly as the painful memories had washed over her she dismissed them and smiled in that homely way she had. She was well liked in this community and kept in touch with many of her protégé's, as she liked to call them. She had aided their arrival into this world and felt she had played a big part on their starting of life. As she put on her coat, hat, scarf and gloves she thought ahead of her day but more importantly she was looking forward to a nice cup of tea in her warm parlour, with that she opened the door and was gone into the still foggy morning. As she walked she was pleased with her work tonight and thrilled for the Fenwick's, she knew how hard times had been for them and now they were complete they had their own little family unit.

Chapter 3

The days passed into weeks and the weeks passed into years, fifteen years passed in which William and Briony had adjusted to the role of parents, they adored their daughter and she them, they had named her Eliza after Briony's grandmother. She had been the most placid baby, a happy child and was now blooming into the early approaches of a young lady, she was tall and slender but in a robust way, had long strawberry blonde hair and the brightest jade green eyes, her young body was developing with curves and she was an exquisite, beautiful young lady. Her colouring she inherited from her mother but her tall, robust characteristics were from her father she had the best combination of both her parents. Like William she had a stubborn streak but had also inherited her mother's kindly, gentle demeanour. She stood in front of the mirror and twirled making her dress swirl around her legs; it was a modest dress, just long enough, but just clingy enough to show her perfect curves. She smiled at her reflection and her hand fluttered to her heart as she tried to control the nervous butterflies that fluttered within. She was going on a date with Luke Barton, an up and coming face but fair, he was an Adonis to Eliza. He was toned, had dirty blond hair which he kept short and neat but ultimately he had the loveliest brown eyes which twinkled amber when he smiled, a girl could fall in love with those eyes alone. Every time she saw him he took her breath away and an unfamiliar warmth would spread down her body giving her the urge to reach out and touch, she was both nervous and excited at the prospect of going out with him, fleetingly she felt a wave of guilt at the lie she had told her parents regarding who she was going out with. They thought she was meeting up with Shelley her best mate; they had been friends and co-conspirators since they had first met when they were both four. Shelley had tried to talk Eliza out of it but she was smitten, she knew her parents would be angry and disappointed with her, but she just had to see him.

Chapter 4

Eliza nervously waited for Luke outside the Dog and Duck public house, she was slightly early and kept glancing up and down the street looking for his car, a tap on her shoulder startled her, spinning round she came face to face with the Adonis that was Luke Barton. He smiled down at her and leaned in to peck her on the cheek, her heart skipped a beat and her cheek burned where his lips had brushed it. When he spoke she nearly swooned with both nervousness and joy.

"You ready, Lizzy? Is it OK if I call you Lizzy?"

Finding her tongue she muttered a response to which he laughed and reaching for her hand led her along the street to a dark blue BMW, he unlocked the door and guided her inside before running around to the driver's side. He turned to her and looking appreciatively he asked her where she would like to go.

"I don't mind," she responded.

"I thought we could go and have a bite to eat, there's a nice little Italian a couple of miles from here, what do you think?" he asked.

Suddenly remembering she had not eaten since breakfast she felt really hungry, "That would be lovely," she responded.

Turning on the engine he looked at her once more and said, "OK, Mamma's Bistro it is then and by the way you look absolutely stunning, gal."

They drove off down the road, Lizzy looking out of the window and thanking God for being noticed by the gorgeous Luke. Ten minutes later they pulled into a carpark, Luke killed the engine and came round to her side to open the door, taking his hand she stepped out of the car, she was standing so close to him and could smell the muskiness of his scent momentarily she closed her eyes and breathed him in. When she opened them he was looking at her with those twinkling amber eyes, he lowered his head and gently kissed her lips, she parted them slightly holding her breath and felt that familiar warmth he instilled within her flush her face and body. For a moment they both stood there looking at each other and Luke knew he had found something very special in this exquisite specimen of a young woman.

Chapter 5

Luke Barton was the son of Arthur and Enid Barton; his had not been a happy childhood, his father was either in the nick or on the piss. His mother was his rock she had single handily raised him and his four younger brothers and none of them went without love from her although the beatings from his father had become worse over time until he just upped and disappeared one day never to return, the family home was poor but a now happy home. There were rumours that Arthur had upset the wrong crowd and he was lying at the bottom of the Thames but no one knew for certain and frankly Luke didn't care. Luke was good with his fists and held no fear of anyone but he was also kind and gentle not to mention his wicked sense of humour, he worked hard and took home a good earn of which he made sure his mum had enough money to look after the family. He was now nineteen and was working his way up the proverbial ladder; he worked for one of the local faces, Gerry McGuire, who was a huge hulk of a man formally from Ireland many years ago. Gerry had a soft spot for young Luke and had taken him under his wing, he saw great potential in Luke and a rare sense of loyalty which he valued in this day and age where someone would knife you or shoot you without so much as a by or leave. It was Gerry who had given Luke his break into the life of a face and the many privileges and respect that came with it. Luke was usually seen by Gerry's side in most business deals, he appreciated the lad's honesty and quick thinking. Luke was good with figures something Gerry had no aptitude for. Gerry knew he would go far, he was well liked by all manner of people, his fairness left him in good stead, Gerry knew he was smitten by the Fenwick girl and had to admit she was a pretty wee thing but hoped Luke was not getting in over his head, the Fenwick's were middle class and considered the slum life in which Luke had been bought up in beneath them, they were by no means haughty but considered bigger and better things for their little girl, understandable as she was their only child.

Chapter 6

Once Lizzy and Luke were seated the waitress came over and took their drinks order, a coke for Luke as he rarely drank and Lizzy opted for a non-alcoholic cocktail. Lizzy looked around her at the quaint authentic restaurant with its low music and soft candlelight, it really was a lovely romantic setting. They chatted over their drinks and when the waitress returned to take their order they ordered a shared starter and their main plus a bottle of house white to drink with their meal. Lizzy was in awe at the luck she was blessed with; she was sitting here with the most handsome man in the room. Their food arrived and Luke poured them both a glass of chilled wine. Lizzy picked up her glass and sipped the delicate wine which warmed her through, her nerves were dissipating and she relaxed enjoying the atmosphere and the light hearted chatter. After they had eaten, a chubby man with a jovial face came over to say hello to Luke, he was the owner and knew who Luke was, but then not many didn't. He chatted for a few minutes and then moved on to the next table. Fabio liked to welcome all his patrons especially the good tippers and commended himself on his friendly restaurant and his top class food as his rounded belly could confirm!

Chapter 7

The bill arrived and Luke paid. He rose and took Lizzy's hand leading her back to the carpark, on this warm evening the air was balmy and a light wind waved her hair around her face making her look almost angelical although her thoughts were neither angelical nor pure. As Luke pulled out of the carpark he turned to Lizzy and asked her what time she needed to be back,

"10.30 will be OK," she replied.

It was only 9.30 and Luke decided to take her for a drive as it was such a pleasant evening, they drove for about fifteen minutes and then Luke pulled over onto a track that led to the infamous lover's lane, he found a nice spot and turned off the engine. He turned to Lizzy and could not really believe his luck that she had agreed to go out with him; she was just so beautiful in every way, especially by the way her dress clung to her curves.

"Have you had a nice evening?" he asked her.

"Yes, absolutely lovely thank you," she replied, his hand crept over hers and he gently lifted her finger to his lips kissing each one individually. Her breath hitched and she closed her eyes savouring the feel of his lips, when she opened them again he was watching her.

"What?" she asked.

"You really are beautiful, Lizzy and I would really like to see you again if you would like to."

Her heart jumped a beat and she reached over to him and kissed him full on his lips, he responded and soon they were both breathless with the force of the passion that flowed between them, Luke felt himself harden and pulled away, he was not going to ruin this and jump her in his car; he respected her and wanted it to be perfect when they did. Yes, he'd had many one-night stands it was par for the course in his job, women throwing themselves at him but this young girl was different, he felt different, felt it in his heart. Lizzy was watching him wondering what he was thinking, had she kissed well enough. Should she move things on? As a virgin she was an amateur at this. Oh she'd kissed boys, but that's what they were, just boys, Luke was a man. She was naïve but she knew what happens between a man and a women, girls talked but knowing and doing were two different things, she didn't feel nervous as such, she knew she wanted this man in every way possible.

"Well?" he said startling her out of her reverie.

"Well what?" she responded.

"Do you want to see me again then?" he asked.

Yes, yes, yes! her insides screamed but she coyly looked at him and said, "Yes, I would like that very much."

Luke let out a breath he hadn't realised he was holding and grinning from ear to ear he folded her into his arms and kissed her with a passion he didn't know he had.

Chapter 8

They drove back to the Dog and Duck chatting away, he pulled over and switched off the engine, turning in his seat he looked at her and asked her why he couldn't drop her off at home?

"My parents don't know I've been on a date, they think I'm with my mate at the local disco, I need to work up to telling them," she replied.

"Are you ashamed to admit you went out with me?" he asked her, suddenly feeling out of his depth.

"Of course not, they are over protective and don't think I should be dating until I'm older, I hate lying to them, but I have a life and I want to live it."

She knew her father would not be happy Luke's reputation preceded him, being a face and her father had no time for the life he lived but she wanted this man in her life and she would be sixteen in a couple of months then they couldn't stop her but she needed to keep this her secret until then. Luke was pleased she wanted him in her life but he hated the deceit, he wanted to shout from the rooftops that she was his girl now but he would give her the time she needed to sort things at home.

"OK, so what about Sunday, can you get away late afternoon and spend that and the evening with me?"

"I would love to," she replied.

With that she opened the door but before she had the chance to get out he was there at her side helping her onto the pavement. He circled his arms around her and kissed her lips, gently at first then harder more inquisitively gently pushing his tongue into her sweet mouth, when they parted he was breathing heavily his erection straining against his jeans. Lizzy had felt it pushing against her, but it only added to the passion building in her, she reached up and cupped his face in her hands, kissing him one last time before turning and starting the short distance towards home.

"Here, Sunday, 3.30?" he shouted after her. She turned, smiled and with a wave of her hand turned the corner. As Luke got back behind the wheel he knew he had found the girl for him and he would protect her until the day he died. If anyone ever hurt her he would without a doubt kill that person with an ease that surprised even him.

Chapter 9

Over the weeks Luke's and Lizzy's relationship blossomed, they spent as much time as possible together enjoying getting to know one another, there had been some heavy petting and intimacy but Luke was determined they would wait until Lizzy turned sixteen, he had big plans for that night. Obviously Lizzy would be spending the night of her birthday with her parents; they had planned a big party to celebrate her coming into womanhood so Luke had secretly made plans of his own. He had booked them into a lovely quaint hotel in Brighton for the weekend; Gerry had helped with the financial aspect as a birthday gift for Lizzy. Luke had told Lizzy she needed to be free Saturday and Sunday which she being forever inquisitive kept trying to prise it out of him as to what they were going to be doing but no matter how much she coerced him with her touching and teasing he managed to keep the surprise a secret from her. He loved Lizzy with all his heart and hoped she felt the same way although neither had spoken of love he felt the special bond they had was as strong for her as it was for him. He had bought her a beautiful silver locket for her birthday, one day he wanted to make her his wife, but for the moment they needed to enjoy life and more importantly speak to her parents, he wanted to let them know his intentions were nothing short of honourable and that he would love, cherish and protect their only daughter. Understandably he was nervous about this prospect but with Gerry's encouragement and knowledge that they were good people he looked forward to no more secrecy, they could come out as a couple without being afraid of getting seen.

Chapter 10

The night of the party had arrived, Lizzy was upstairs getting ready for her party, she had carefully applied her make-up and her hair had been unravelled from the rags she had slept in the night before, her hair now hung in a cascade of curls flowing down her back and gathering around her face, what with her make-up and hair she looked like an Angel. Her mother poked her head around the door to tell her that she had half an hour before the guests were due to start arriving, Lizzy thanked her and stared back at her reflection in the mirror, sighing her mind wandered to Luke. She had managed to grab a couple of hours with him yesterday between party preparation and his work, Lizzy knew what Luke did and she had met Gerry several times, she had really taken to him and he had charmed her with his Irish banter and joviality. Luke had bought her a beautiful silver locket with a picture of them both inside where he had gotten her picture from was a surprise but she suspected Shelley had a hand in it. Shelley had started to date one of Luke's friends, Aaron, so they had been on many double dates; they all got on very well and made a handsome foursome. Lizzy was going to wear the locket tonight and never take it off, to her it was a declaration of Luke's love and would always sit close to her heart, her heart gave a flutter as she thought about their weekend away next week, she knew they were going somewhere as Shelley was covering for her as had been pre-planned but she had no idea where, that much neither of them would tell her. She felt intrigued and excited, they had kissed and caressed, gently touching each other but had not made love. Luke wanted to wait and now finally the night would come and frankly Lizzy could not wait, she loved Luke so much and wanted to give herself to him. The feelings his kisses and caresses evoked in her were so mind blowing she wanted to feel him inside her, for him to take her nipples in his mouth and tease, she wanted to touch him to hold his manhood in her hands and pleasure him. As she closed her eyes and thought of the two of them together, naked, entwined in each other's arms her breathing quickened and her hand wandered down to the parting in her robe where she gently touched herself, surprised to find she was wet, her breath caught and she shivered as she imagined Luke's hand gently caressing her swollen bud, she could feel that familiar rise of pleasure that had before amazed her at the way her body submitted to his touch, now as she put more pressure to herself she could feel that pleasure increasing and just as she felt herself becoming lost in that pleasure a sharp rap on the door broke the moment and Lizzy jumped as the rap was followed by her mother shouting ten minutes through the closed door. Lizzy gasped and opened her eyes, the face that looked back was flushed and Lizzy thought a little embarrassed. She had never touched herself before; she was not naïve and completely in the dark when it came to sex but had never felt the urge. The feelings Luke brought out in her both intrigued and frightened her but not in a bad way. She knew she would give herself to him willingly and felt wanton at the thought but excited at the prospect.

"Look what you do to me, Luke Barton," she whispered to the empty room and with a shake of her head, which set her curls bouncing, she proceeded to get dressed.

Chapter 11

In exactly ten minutes a more composed Lizzy was just coming down the stairs as the doorbell rang, her mother glanced up as she walked across the foyer to answer the door waving away the help they had employed for the night she wanted to welcome her guests into her home, a home she was very proud of, she stopped and stared, her precious daughter had indeed flowered into a beautiful young lady.

"Lizzy, darling, you look stunning! William come here and look at our very glamorous daughter."

William appeared from the parlour a scotch in his hand and looked up, wow he breathed this beautiful young woman was his daughter and she was a sight to see. Lizzy carried on down the stairs and looked from one of her parents to the other smiling at the effect she knew she was having on them both, she looked and felt amazing and she knew that in a meek way.

"I'll get the door shall I while you two just stand there!" and at that she opened the door. The party soon livened up, there was a continual supply of champagne being brought around by a waiter and a waitress also a never-ending supply of nibbles to suit everyone's taste, the atmosphere was pleasant and light hearted with everyone chatting in various groups. The evening went perfectly with the birthday cake and toasts out of the way it was soon midnight and guests were beginning to leave in dribs and drabs, Lizzy flopped onto the two seater under the big bay window next to Shelley, she was staying the night and the girls already had a stash of champagne and nibbles in Lizzy's room for their own late night party, they had been secretly sneaking upstairs on several occasions with their hoard. When the last of the guests had gone Lizzy thanked her parents for a wonderful party and the girls excused themselves and headed up the stairs to their room.

Shelley and Lizzy discarded their dresses and donned nightshirts, they grabbed their stash and plonked themselves down on the bed, Lizzy poured them both a glass of champagne offered one to Shelley and grabbed a sausage roll, as she sat munching Shelley sighed and looking at Lizzy she smiled.

"What are you smiling at?" Lizzy asked her.

"It was a fantastic party, Liz," Shelley replied, "and you looked great." Reaching out she took the locket in her fingers and asked, "Do you like it?"

"Oh Shell, it's beautiful," Lizzy replied. The girls chatted about Luke and the upcoming weekend, Aaron, make up, clothes and sex until finally exhausted they climbed under the blankets and fell asleep each with their own dreamy thoughts.

Chapter 12

The next week went so slowly that Lizzy thought she would die of excitement, she was due to start her nurse training in a couple of weeks so had very little to occupy her, she helped in the kitchen with baking, tried to read but couldn't concentrate on the story so had given up on that one, now she was wandering in the garden relishing the warmth of the sun, her mother was the gardener and the garden did look very pretty and colourful with all the flowers in bloom. It was Thursday and now she had only two more days to wait until Saturday when she was meeting Luke, she had missed him terribly as due to work they hadn't seen each other since the night before her party. She smiled at the thought of being with him for two whole days and a night, a nervous flutter somersaulted in her tummy as she thought about that night, she was not nervous about being alone with him, but what if he didn't like what he saw or what if I don't know what to do and he thinks I'm useless in bed? Dismissing the thought she chided herself for being negative, besides there was nothing wrong with the way she looked!

Chapter 13

Finally the morning of Saturday arrived; Lizzy packed her overnight bag and headed down for breakfast. Her father was reading the paper and looked up as she arrived.

"You ready for the off?" he asked.

"Yes," Lizzy replied.

"Do you want me to drop you off at Shelley's?" he offered.

"No, it's fine thank you. I'm fine to walk to meet her," Lizzy responded.

God, I hate lying to my parents she mused, but after this weekend I will tell them and introduce them to Luke. After breakfast she kissed her parents goodbye amidst promises of staying safe and behaving, they thought she was going to Shelley's cousins for the weekend in the country, Shelley was going so there was no fear of her being seen around until Sunday, grabbing her bag she donned her jacket and was out of the door, excitement fuelling her forward. She was so looking forward to seeing Luke after what seemed like an eternity since she last felt his arms around her and his lips on hers. She rounded the corner and there he was leaning against his car watching for her, she quickened her pace and walked into his outstretched arms for a warm embrace.

"Ready?" he breathed into her hair as he savoured the scent of her, fresh lemon soap and her own musky, heady scent. "God I've missed you Lizzy, are you sure you are OK with this, us going away?" She drew back, looked him in the eyes and he could see the love and passion in her sparkling eyes, there was no need for words. With that he took her bag and placed it in the boot, he opened the car door and helped her in to the passenger seat then ran around to the driver's side where he started the engine and they were off. The sun was shining and it was a lovely warm morning promising to be a wonderful day as they drove he asked her about the party and what she had been doing with her week, was she looking forward to nursing school? She in turn asked him about his week. As they neared Brighton she glimpsed the sea and turning to him enquired as to where they were going, he turned to look at her and announced, "We are going to Brighton and staying in a lovely small hotel on the sea front, are you nervous?"

She looked straight at him and firmly said, "No, are you?"

"A little," he confessed, he had thought of nothing else for days. He was excited but apprehensive, what if he hurt her or she didn't like it, he was not a virgin and had slept with some stunning women as was par for the course in his way of life, but never with these feelings of pure love he felt for Lizzy, he knew he was to be her first and this thought made him happy, she was and would always be his Lizzy, he knew she was inexperienced but he would show her the way, he wanted this to be perfect and all his planning would make it perfect, he hoped. They pulled up outside the quirky, quaint hotel and he killed the engine taking her hand he gently kissed her fingers.

"You ready, Mrs Barton?" he laughingly asked her, to which she giggled and leaned forward to kiss him passionately on the lips.

"Ready," she said.

They got out of the car, Luke retrieved their bags and led her into the small reception where a young woman looked up and greeted them. She was a ruddy-faced, well-rounded, jovial woman with laughter dancing in her eyes.

"We have a room reserved for tonight under Mr and Mrs Barton," he told her.

Smiling, she checked the register, "Oh yes," she responded, "We have you booked into one of our more exclusive rooms with a sea view, is that suitable for you both?"

"That will be fantastic, thanks," Luke replied, he took the proffered key, refused help with the bags and led Lizzy up the stairs to the first floor and along the corridor to room thirteen. At the door he turned to Lizzy and, hooking his arm around her waist, surmised, "Well unlucky for some, but definitely lucky for us – beautiful!" He unlocked the door and stood back for her to enter the room.

"Oh, Luke, it's absolutely lovely," Lizzy said as she took in the room with its four poster bed and oldie worldly décor, there was even their own bathroom and the view was stupendous, the sea shone in the bright sunshine an azure blue, perfect, well more than perfect. Luke followed her in and placed the bags on the blanket box at the end of the bed, he caught her from behind and wrapped his arms around her resting his head on her shoulder and sighed a contented sigh.

"What do you want to do first?" he asked her. "Lunch?"

She nodded, not trusting herself to speak as the emotions running through her left her at a loss for words.

Chapter 14

They locked the door, strolled back downstairs and out into the bright light of the sunny afternoon, they wandered down towards the sea front until they found a lovely, welcoming café where they took a seat outside and waited for the waitress to take their order. Lizzy ordered a water and prawn salad, Luke opted for pie and mushy peas with a glass of coke, they chatted and ate in relative ease both enjoying the others company, they felt so comfortable in each other's company sometimes words were not needed, the silence was a comfortable one, both their minds were on the forthcoming evening a mixture of emotions but at no point had either of them any regret at where they were now and where this would go. Lizzy broke the silence, "Why does the food taste so much nicer here?" she mused.

She was indeed right thought Luke and replied, "I think it is a mixture of everything, the weather, the setting, my girl sitting here with me as pretty as a picture…."

Lizzy blushed and reached for his hand, "Let's go exploring," she said, rising from her chair.

They spent a wonderful afternoon together walking down the quaint cobbled streets, they sat on the warm, golden sand eating cockles and then ice creams watching families playing and swimming, fishermen going about their usual business and as dusk began to fall they walked hand in hand back to the hotel. Back in their room they both changed and headed out for an evening meal, Luke ready first nipped down to reception and ordered a bottle of bubbles to be put in their room on ice for when they returned, the receptionist gave him a knowing smile to which Luke blushed and nodded his thanks. On his return back to the room Lizzy was ready, wearing a summery, pastel, flowy dress and she had piled her beautiful locks in a messy bun on top of her head, walking behind her he kissed her slender neck, took her hand and led her back out onto the street. They headed for a nice little Italian they had seen on their travels earlier in the day. Once seated the waiter handed them menus and a complimentary glass of champagne, they perused the menu and Lizzy opted for Mussels in a creamy sauce, Luke opted for a steak. The food arrived and he ordered a bottle of the house white.

"Lizzy, are you having a nice time?" he asked her, to which she replied.

"Luke, I am having the best time ever and the best thing is not having to look over our shoulders in case we are seen and reported back to my parents, this is pure bliss!"

Luke felt as contented as she did and thanked his lucky stars that she had chosen him, he could not imagine his life without her in it and knew he would do anything for this girl, anything. How ironic that this thought would come back to haunt him. They enjoyed a most pleasant evening, eating, drinking, talking, listening to the soft music and soaking up the relaxed atmosphere. Eventually they paid the bill and wandered back down the cobbled street towards the hotel; the stars shone bright in the night sky illuminating the shapes of the fishing boats anchored at the dock bobbing around on the current; other couples wandered past and smiled, each holding hands, with a sense of togetherness that this idyllic, romantic place induced.

Chapter 15

They arrived back at the hotel and made their way up to the room both immersed in their own thoughts, the nerves had set in slightly mixed in with anticipation, excitement, longing and the knowledge that this was it, they entered their room which was bathed in soft light, the drapes were drawn and the bed had been turned down, on the table sat a bucket with the champagne on ice, next to that were strawberries and two ornately styled champagne flutes. Whoever had delivered the champagne had thoughtfully set the scene. Luke took Lizzy's jacket and then poured them both a glass of champagne, he turned to her and their eyes met, she smiled rather coyly and moved forward so that they were closer, but not physically touching, her hand reached up and cupped the side of his face, he leant in and kissed her, slowly at first then as she responded his kiss became more probing his tongue explored her mouth savouring the tangy taste of garlic and champagne, her arms pulled his head down as she sought his mouth more passionately, when they pulled apart they were both breathing heavily, their faces flushed from the intensity of their feelings.

"Are you sure this is what you want?" he huskily whispered

She cocked her head to one side and eyed him smiling lazily, "Yes, I've never felt more sure about anything. I love you, Luke, and I want to love you," she replied.

His response was to kiss her again this time more deeply than the last, he traced the line of her neck, her skin feeling hot to his touch and reaching for the zip of her dress he slowly pulled it down, it fell around her feet and she stood there in her lacy cream underwear her tanned legs dark in contrast to the creamy lace, her breath caught as she watched him looking at her, she did not feel shy but happy at the appreciating look on his face. Lizzy reached out and slowly unbuttoned his shirt then tossed it onto the chair, he reached for her crushing her body to his as his lips again sought the warmth of her mouth swollen from kissing, she gasped and held him to her savouring the feel of his bare chest on her heated skin, her hand sought his belt and began to unbuckle it aware of the hardness of him as she strove to manoeuvre the belt away from his trouser button and zip, slowly she lowered his zip and he moaned into her mouth. She felt his hands reach behind her to undo the clasp of her bra, he released her breasts, heavy with want her nipples straining forward begging to be touched, as if reading her mind he lowered his head and gently sucked on one nipple then the other while grasping her breasts in his hands, she moaned and her body jerked, she could feel her wetness such was the extent of the passion flowing between them like an electrical current searching for its point of contact. He gently laid her on the bed and removed his trousers and underwear, he then lay down beside her, his head propped up on his elbow so that he could gaze at her laid before him, her hand reached out and caressed his taut muscles, she wandered down, her fingers moving over his body like hot needles, his erection strained, god how he wanted to be inside her, she wrapped her hand around his erection and stroked him, he grew bigger and her eyes widened in surprise. Taking her hand he moved in closer raising her arms above her head, holding them there while kissing her with a hunger to which she responded. She could feel his erection pressing against her and gasped as he took her eager nipple into his mouth rolling his tongue around the tender area, his hand caressed her skin as his fingers sought her sex.

"You're so wet," he whispered against her breast the warm breath sending shudders through her body. His fingers sought her gently at first then harder as he stroked and added pressure, his fingers moved down and stroked the slickness of her, dipping a finger into her and penetrating her softly, her eyes fluttered closed and her hips began to move against his palm as he rubbed her while gently fingering her, she reached down and her fingers encircled his cock moving her hand up and down, he bit down on her nipple and her back arched up towards him crushing herself to his chest.

"I want you, want you inside me," she whispered to him, he kissed her and positioning himself above her he gently guided the moist tip of his cock to her opening. Lizzy opened her legs wider and thrust her hips up to meet him, he sank into her and she groaned; he looked at her seeking permission to thrust deeper into her and she nodded. She wanted him so much that at first there had been a sting of pain as he had first entered her, but as he moved inside her and she moved with him a feeling of excitement and ecstasy overtook all thoughts as she strove to take him deeper and deeper reaching out for that moment where she knew all control would be lost, fire was running through her and with a moan she held onto him for dear life as her orgasm shot through her with such a power her whole body shuddered and shook. As Luke felt her muscles tighten and contract around him he could hold on no longer and his release exploded through him, her muscles still contracting kept his orgasm going for what seemed never ending then as her body sank beneath him he collapsed on top of her, both breathing hard. He rolled off her fearing his weight would crush her and enveloped her into his arms, they lay there for what seemed an age, their eyes closed, reliving the sheer ecstasy they had evoked in each other.

Lizzy broke the silence, "I love you, Luke," she said.

He turned to lazily look at her and replied, "I love you too, Lizzy."

Then he laughed and she looked at him puzzled. "What?"

He kissed her and said, "I am the luckiest man alive, you are laying with me naked as the day you were born looking like a beautiful Angel in fact you are my Angel and that is what I will call you," Lizzy looked at him and smiled, her fate was sealed, she would be his wife, have his children and do this every day, that would be heaven to her. Luke rose and brought over the champagne, passing one glass to her and getting back on the bed he pulled the throw over them and Lizzy snuggled into him, they drank champagne, ate strawberries and talked about their plans for the future, sated and happy they fell asleep in each other's arms their bodies entwined.

Chapter 16

Lizzy stretched and as the events of the previous night entered her sleep fuddled mind she smiled, turning over she opened her eyes and found Luke propped up on his elbow watching her, he leant down and kissed her full lips, "Mmmmmm," she sighed, as his kiss became more insistent. She felt the stirrings of passion and she responded by pressing herself to him relishing the warmth of his body as he became hard, she reached down and wrapped her hand around his erection. He rolled on top of her and nuzzled her neck feathering it with tiny kisses as he moved down her body, taking her nipple into his mouth he sucked gently while his hand found her moist and ready for him, she moaned as he lazily circled her clit with his thumb the sensation hardening the little bud. Her breath hitched in her throat and as her hips jerked her orgasm shot through her with a force she barely thought possible, Luke continued his slow circling motion until she had stilled, he looked down at her his beautiful Angel as she lay beneath him her hair fanned out on the pillow and he felt the weight of his love in his heart. So lost in his thoughts, he was jerked back to reality as her hand began caressing his erection, she eased herself from under him and sat astride him gently moving herself over his cock, with laboured breathing he manoeuvred her onto the tip of his cock and gently pushed inside her, she gasped and held him tight inside her, together they moved as one as he held her hips and ground himself into her, he could feel her orgasm close as her muscles contracted and, needing no more encouragement, he let go as she came spilling his seed into her. She collapsed on top of him as her orgasm calmed and he wrapped his arms around her holding her tightly to him, here they lay while their breathing slowed and the beating of their hearts calmed. Luke pushed her hair from her face and kissed her tenderly.

"Well, Angel what would you like to do today?" he asked.

"I'm starving," she replied, "so dress and then a wander out for some breakfast?" she suggested.

Giggling she left the bed and went into the bathroom and turning on the taps proceeded to run a bath, he joined her and encircled her in his arms savouring the sweet smell of her. An hour later they were bathed, dressed and ready for breakfast, hand in hand they left the room and went down to reception and out into the warm sunny morning, they wandered for a while and then chanced upon a café down one of the endless cobbled roads, they entered and took a table in the window. The waitress came over and took their order, a pot of tea, bacon and eggs for Luke, toast and marmalade for Lizzy. After they had eaten they headed down to the seafront and sat watching the fisherman unloading their catch of the morning, neither spoke for a while but they didn't need to the silence was not awkward but a happy one as they sat together holding hands and admiring the view. Lizzy broke the silence.

"Do you know, Luke, I could quite happily live somewhere like this, it's so beautiful and peaceful."

"It's our little hideaway, Angel," he replied. "But I'm sorry to be the bearer of bad news, we really do need to leave soon, Angel, I promised Shelley you would be back by late afternoon."

With a contented sigh she turned to him, kissed him and pulled him to his feet, "Come on then, I'll race you down the beach," and with that she turned and ran off.

Chapter 17

As they neared London they found a country pub and stopped for lunch, they sat out in the pub garden and demolished sandwiches washed down with shandy. Happy and full they continued on their journey back to the smog of the city with its cloying smells of city life. Luke pulled up outside Shelley's house and she came out to greet them as Luke came round to open the door for Lizzy, she stepped out and he kissed her before going to the boot to retrieve her bag. After swapping pleasantries with Shelley he kissed Lizzy one more time, hugged her to him and then drove off to meet up with Gerry and work. Lizzy watched him go, smiling at the memories of the last two days firmly etched in her mind. Shelley tugged her arm and dragged her up the steps and into the house, "I want to hear all about it," she said, "I'll make a pot of tea and we can have a chat."

Chapter 18

A couple of hours later Lizzy was home and up in her room when her mum tapped on the door, "Come in," she called. Briony entered the room and gazed at her daughter, she looked different but Briony couldn't place why? "The country air seems to agree with you, darling," she said. "You look all flushed and lovely."

"Oh, Mum, it was lovely and so nice to get out of the city for a while," Lizzy replied, "I had a fantastic time!"

"Oh good," Briony replied. "Dinner will be ready in ten minutes," and with that she was gone leaving Lizzy alone. Lizzy suddenly felt nervous, she knew that her parents were not going to be happy, but they needed to know she had met the man of her dreams and she was in love, she was going to tell them tonight over dinner then it was all out in the open and they wouldn't need to hide the fact they were together, her parents would love Luke, he was charming, caring, handsome, he wasn't poor and he looked after her; but he was a local face and that fact was what made her nervous, she wasn't sure how her parents would feel about that but she was sixteen now and it was her choice who she wanted to be with. When she came down both her parents were already sitting in the parlour at the table and her mum was serving food onto their plates, she sat down and they ate in silence, she toyed with her food suddenly having no appetite, wondering how she was going to broach the subject.

"You alright, Lizzy?" her father asked.

Lizzy looked at her father and then at her mother, clearing her throat she spoke "I have met someone," she said, her parents looked up and watched her, waiting for her to continue. "His name is Luke Barton and he is so lovely, he treats me like a queen and he is so handsome. Mum, you will love him."

"I see," her father replied. "Does he work, and how old is he?"

"He is a little older than me and yes he has a job and earns good money," she replied.

"Where does he work?" her father asked.

Lizzy hesitated, looked at her father and said, "He works for Gerry McGuire."

Her father stared at her and calmly said, "I forbid you to see him anymore."

For a minute Lizzy thought she had misheard him then realising what he had just said opened her mouth to protest, but her father continued, "No daughter of mine is going out with a villain, I forbid it while you are under my roof. What is wrong with you, girl? Have we not brought you up better than this? My daughter hanging about with villains and God knows who."

Lizzy just looked at him and then she looked to her mother who sat there her face unreadable, "But…"

"That is the end of the matter, you will not see him again, do you hear me, girl? This is my house and you will do as I say," her father said to her. He pushed away from the table and left the room.

Lizzy stared after him while his words sank in, she turned to her mother, "Mum, will you talk to him please?" desperation now filling her.

"I can't, Lizzy, because I agree with him, we have such high hopes for you and a gangster's wife is not one of them! You will not see him again," with that she collected the tray and began piling the dinner plates on it, then she, too, left the room and Lizzy could hear her moving around the kitchen.

For what seemed an age Lizzy just sat there her emotions in turmoil, she loved her parents dearly, but she loved Luke so much and her heart ached for him, what would she do? Surely they would come round, but she knew she was grasping at straws her father would never change his mind, she knew that once he made his mind up that was it and nothing would sway him. With a heavy heart she went to her room and throwing herself down on her bed she sobbed. Eventually worn out from crying Lizzy fell asleep but the dreams that invaded her were not happy ones, she saw Luke in the distance holding his arms open to her, but she couldn't go to him she was unable to move, when she broke free it was to see her father grabbing for her to prevent her from going to him, she awoke with a start her head heavy with all the crying she had done. She lay there listening to the house coming to life as her mother banged around in the kitchen. She rose and knew exactly what she was going to do. She washed, dressed, tied her hair up in a bun and dragged her case from under the bed. When she had packed enough for a few days she placed her case by the door and went down for breakfast, her father sat across from her his face stony as he did his best to ignore the fact that his only daughter had obviously been crying for an age by the look of her swollen red eyes, when he had finished he rose and left for work. Lizzy looked across to her mother and saw no sympathy there, she knew if she wanted to spend her life with Luke then she had to leave because being without him was a thought so unbearable she was not prepared to even contemplate it, with her mind made up she went back to her room to wait for her mother to go to her usual coffee morning at the church.

With the house silent, Lizzy crept downstairs to make sure she had gone and finding her mother's coat and hat gone she ran back upstairs and collected her things, she walked out of the front door and looking back with tears in her eyes she walked off. Her first stop was Shelley's house whose parents thankfully were also out, Shelley ushered her in and Lizzy burst into tears, her friend hugged her as she sobbed and when she had finally quieted they talked. Shelley knew how her friend felt about Luke and she was heartfelt sorry for the situation she was in but her parents would never agree to letting Lizzy stay she knew that not after what had happened with her parents.

"What are you going to do, Liz?" she asked her.

"I don't know," Lizzy replied. They talked through possibilities, but Lizzy had no money so renting somewhere was not an option. Finally, Lizzy conceded she would have to ring Luke; she picked up the phone and dialled the number Luke had given her, after several rings the phone was answered by Gerry.

"Can I speak to Luke please?" she asked him.

"He is not here, darling," Gerry replied. "He's out doing a bit of collecting for me, but he won't be long, shall I get him to call you back?"

"No it's fine, can you ask him to come to Shelley's house please?" Lizzy asked him.

"Ah to be sure I will, are you OK?" Gerry responded, Lizzy felt the tears spring into her eyes and swallowing a sob she mumbled her goodbyes and Gerry promised to send him round as soon as he was back.

Chapter 19

Lizzy spent the morning with Shelley talking about what her plans were, she was due to start at the hospital for her nurse training the following week and that would bring some money in making her self-sufficient at least, but for the moment she had no idea where to go or what to do, so until she had spoken to Luke it was all left up in the air.

Finally there was a knock at the door. Shelley answered it and came back with Luke in tow. Lizzy fell into his arms sobbing, he held her close stroking her hair as she sobbed into his shoulder. When she had calmed down he sat down with her on the couch and she told him what had happened and that she had left her parent's home but had nowhere to go and how sorry she was to bring him into this mess.

"Well, my Angel, we will just have to find you somewhere to stay. I'm afraid you can't stay at my old mum's as there is no room and it's not quite what you're used to, but I have an idea," he eventually said. "Come on let's get you in the car and we will get this sorted out, OK?"

Lizzy nodded, wiped her eyes and Shelley fetched her coat, she hugged her friend with a promise of letting her know where she would be. Luke drove to the Blue Diamond club one of Gerry's many business ventures and they climbed the narrow stairs up to the office, Gerry was on the phone having a heated conversation as they arrived, he gestured them in and finished his call. He came around the desk and hugged Lizzy, then after guiding her into a chair he sat back behind his antique mahogany desk. He loved this room with its manly décor, it had a cosy feel about it and God knows he spent enough time here; this was where he conducted most of his business dealings from.

"I'll have a scotch, lad, as you're nearest to the cabinet. Lizzy, would you like a drink? You look like you could do with one, gal."

"I'm fine thanks, Gerry," she replied. Luke handed Gerry his drink and then sat down next to Lizzy in a matching chair, he looked across at Gerry and spoke.

"I have a bit of a favour to ask you, boss."

"What's on your mind, lad?" Gerry asked him,

"Lizzy needs a place to stay do you have anything until I can sort something out?"

Gerry thought for a moment and then smiled. "As it happens I've just acquired the old Grey Dove, you know the club just off the Harringay Road; it has a nice but small flat upstairs. It could do with a nice touch to it and I was going to offer it to you, lad, as I want you to oversee the renovations, I'm thinking of turning it into a new Jazz club with a bit of my usual entertainment, what do you reckon, lad?"

Luke looked at Lizzy and said, "What do you reckon Liz, you think you could cope with me on a bit more of a full time basis?" Lizzy thought for a minute and, smiling, she nodded her acceptance.

"Well that's settled then," said Gerry raising his glass and toasting a new venture. "So what's going on then, have you left home, gal?" he asked Lizzy. She explained the day's events and Gerry listened intently until she had finished. With a sigh he reached for her hand across the desk and gave it a squeeze, "Well you're here now and welcome to the family," he said, Lizzy felt so overwhelmed her eyes filled and a single tear traced its way down her cheek.

"Thank you, Gerry, you are so kind and I am in your debt," she said.

"Ah be away with you, gal, my Luke loves you and that's enough for me, so we'll have no more tears and Luke go downstairs and fetch a bottle of the bubbly stuff we need to toast new ventures and a new life."

Luke left the office and Gerry suggested to Lizzy that while the flat was theirs it would need a bit of work doing on it, painting, new furniture and the like, he would get a couple of his lads onto it and they could move in within the next couple of days, but in the meantime she was coming home with him and could stay in one of the guest rooms, he picked up the phone and rang Hilda his housekeeper to advise her they would be having a couple of house guests for a few days. Just as he came off the phone Luke returned with the champagne and three glasses, he popped the cork, poured them each a glass, and together they chinked glasses and toasted a happy future.

Chapter 20

Lizzy spent three days at Gerry's house, she liked Hilda, she was like the grandmother she had never had and the old woman took her under her wing, Hilda had been with Gerry for the best part of twenty years ever since he arrived in London she knew what his business was and had on more than one occasion been his alibi, but she loved him like a son and he in turn loved her like a mother. He had left Ireland after the fire that had taken his parents, two brothers and his baby sister, everyone knew who was responsible, the Kormarick boys. Gerry's pa had been a well-known name within the criminal fraternity he had always been a fair man but those Kormarick boys had committed the worst sin ever in this game, they had beat up an old man and viciously raped his daughter in front of him then they had torched their small semi to hide the evidence. Gerry's pa had exacted his revenge and there had been a price out for the boys. They had managed to stay off the radar and in doing so had found plenty of time to form a revenge plan. One night believing the coast to be clear they had sneaked out of hiding and had torched the house killing all but Gerry who had been away for the night, his family had not stood a chance, even if they had awoken it would have been useless as the evil Kormarick boys had barricaded both the front and back doors preventing any means of escape for those inside. That night had been the worst of Gerry's life as everyone he cared for had perished in the fire. When Gerry found out he had hunted those boys down and tortured them before killing them. With the Military police on his case he had bought a passage over to England and had come via trawler to London docks where he already had several contacts, as was the nature of their business, he soon became settled into his new life and not long after had found Hilda. Hilda had been a working woman who in her heyday had been a looker but the elements and the game had not been kind to her and she was barely scraping a living together when Gerry took her under his wing and made her mistress of his house in the form of housekeeper and now loyal friend. She sympathised with Lizzy as she, too, had once been in love and similarly been turned out by her parents, but all had not ended well for Hilda, the love of her life as she thought at the time had beaten and abused her in the most malicious way, she had run away and ended up working on the streets to feed herself. Gerry had found her crumpled body on the Tottenham road where she had been beaten and thrown from a car when her punter refused to pay, he nursed her back to health and she had never left, she had dedicated her life to the son she had never had. That morning Luke had rung to say he would be picking Lizzy up at noon and to get packing. Lizzy now sat in the huge kitchen sipping coffee and watching Hilda go about her daily business. Luke arrived on the dot and bounded into the kitchen smiling and swung Lizzy around before putting her back on her feet.

"You ready, Angel?" he asked her. "We are going home, well our home for the time being." Lizzy put on her coat and followed Luke out into the hallway. She turned and hugged Hilda tightly, thanking her for having her, she knew here she had found a friend, then they were out the door into the car and on their way. Luke chatted all the way there about the flat and how cosy it was looking, about the furniture he had bought to put in it and how happy they would be, but most importantly they would be together, his excitement was infectious and she found herself grinning at him as she listened. A moment of sadness crept over her as she thought of her parents and how awful they were being towards her at the moment, she had rung them a couple of evenings ago to tell them she was safe and her father had told her she could come home if she gave up on this silly illusion of being with a villain, sadly Lizzy knew they would never except Luke and they had never even given him a chance. Pushing it to the back of her mind she looked around as Luke pulled into a carpark and drove around the back of the club. The flat was accessible from the club and also from a fire escape that led to the side door, before he could open her door she was already out of the car and looking up at the window framed by a cream net. His arm came around her waist and he propelled her forward and up the stairs, he unlocked the door and holding her hand led her into the hallway. He pushed her up against the wall and kissed her, urgently seeking the warmth of her mouth.

"I've been dying to do this since I picked you up," he breathed. "Welcome home, Angel."

He led her down the hallway to the first door which opened into the bedroom where he put down her case,

"Well, what do you think?" he asked her, she gazed around the room, it had been painted in the palest of blues there was a double bed with a pale blue throw, wardrobe, dressing table and bed side tables, it looked idyllic. Luke came behind her and circled his arms around her, she felt his warm breath on her neck and as he began kissing her she felt the first stirrings of passion mounting in her, she laid her head back to allow him better access to her neck, his arms came around and removed her coat then starting on the buttons of her blouse he slowly began undoing them until he had freed her of it and gazing down at her he whispered, "You are so beautiful, Angel."

Lizzy turned around and kissed him urgently her tongue exploring his mouth, he freed her breasts and cupped them in his hands rolling his thumbs over her erect nipples; he bent his head and sucked hard on one eliciting a groan from her parted lips. Lizzy eased his coat off him and grabbed his erection which was straining at the hindrance of his jeans. He growled deep in his throat and gently pushed her down onto the bed, he knelt before her and removed her shoes, slacks and lacy pants and then easing himself between her legs he bent his head and kissed the tops of her thighs caressing one nipple with his hand while the other slowly, sensually circled her clit. Lizzy whimpered and he bought his mouth down to her mound of perfect golden hair where he teased her with a flick of his tongue, her clit instantly hardened under his breath and her hips jerked upwards wanting more, he inserted a finger inside her and as he licked and sucked her most private area his finger worked her until she could take no more and she came hard quivering beneath his gaze.

"More," she murmured "I want you, want to feel you inside me," Luke didn't need asking twice he stood and discarded his clothes, his cock was huge and throbbing painfully waiting for its release, he entered her and rode her hard, but she matched him move for move and with a cry she came, it was his undoing and as he came the breath was knocked out of him by the force of his orgasm.

Breathing heavily they held each other; Luke kissed her and said, "Welcome home Angel."

Lizzy kissed him and her cheeks were damp, puzzled he feared he had hurt her. "No, far from it, these are tears of joy, I am so happy, Luke, and now here we are in our first home together not to mention christening our first bed!" she told him. He showed her round the rest of the flat, it had been decorated to a very high standard, Gerry had definitely pushed the boat out and the small flat was gorgeous – fit for a queen!

Chapter 21

They spent the next hour or so unpacking their things, just as they had finished there was a knock on the door that led down to the club Luke opened it and there stood Gerry with a bottle of bubbles and three glasses, "Well you young uns I see you're settling in, do you like it?" he asked nervously, he had help from Hilda when it had come to the finer points, the woman stuff and Hilda had not let him down the place was amazing. Lizzy threw her arms around his neck and kissed him.

"Gerry, it's wonderful I don't know how we can ever thank you enough."

Blushing Gerry replied, "Seeing you happy is payment enough, gal." They drank the champagne and then Gerry and Luke went down to sort out some things in the club on the condition that they would return in a couple of hours as Lizzy was cooking them a meal, Hilda had also stocked the fridge and cupboards with enough food to feed an army. Just after six the three of them sat down to a feast. As the evening wore on Gerry made his excuses and left, he was meeting up with a lovely brunette that worked the bar in one of his clubs and damn he was looking forward to peeling her clothes off, she was small, dark and bubbly just his type, he had never married and had no intention of doing so, he was having enough fun without saddling himself with a wife and he was happy as he was, why spoil things. But truth be known Gerry was lonely, not for friends but for that someone special to come home to and hold, he had Hilda but it wasn't the same. Sadly, though, he was not prepared to get involved for fear of being hurt. When his family was murdered it had broken his heart and he didn't know if his heart could take that much pain again.

Chapter 22

Lizzy had written to her parents to let them know she was OK and to make sure they had her new address but six weeks down the line she had not received a reply, at first it had really upset her but now she had resigned herself to the fact that they knew where she was and left it at that. She had started her nursing and was enjoying learning all aspects of what a nurse did, the academic side was hard but she was coping. Life in their little flat was bliss, they had their ups and downs but on the whole they lived together quite happily. Luke's mum was a regular visitor to the little flat and Lizzy liked her a lot, they got on like a house on fire, she was typical East End born and bred, but Lizzy had become used to her course ways and liked her all the more for it. Luke had become very busy out all hours of the day and night but he always came home to Lizzy when his work allowed, he had become Gerry's right hand man, he was fair but when needed he would not be made a mug of and most people who worked with him knew how ruthless he could be when crossed. Gerry looked upon him as the son he had never had and hoped one day to hand the business over to Luke. He knew Luke was well liked which in their line of work was an added bonus but despite his camaraderie he was one of the hardest men Gerry had ever had work for him, hard but fair and that was a good thing in this business, people knew how far they could push him before they overstepped the mark and Luke had respect for everyone he worked with even the lowest of the scum they had dealings with, if the odd one took the piss they knew about it, Luke was by no means a walkover. Lizzy knew what line of work Luke did but she never asked and he never told, he preferred to keep the two separate the less Lizzy knew the less there was to hurt her, at first she had been upset with him due to the fact he spent a lot of time managing Gerry's more lucrative business's, the lap dancing clubs and the brothels, but as the weeks passed she knew that he only had eyes for her and loved her more than his own life, for this she also loved him dearly. She also knew that if anyone hurt her he would commit murders for her regardless, she took no pleasure in this but his protectiveness made her feel loved and safe. This she did not take lightly but nevertheless it made her feel all the more loved and protected.

Chapter 23

It was Sunday night, a week before Christmas and Lizzy was in the kitchen preparing the evening meal for her and Luke, they had spent a lovely day together which was a rarity for both of them albeit they had spent a lot of the day in bed making love, as she cooked her mind wandered and she felt the usual stirrings as she relived the previous few hours laying in Luke's arms sated from the orgasm that had blown her mind. Sex with Luke was out of this world and she felt blessed to have found the right man from the word go; she could not imagine sharing herself with anyone else and feeling the passion she felt with Luke, as if reading her mind he appeared behind her encircling her with his arms and pressing himself against her, she sighed and laid her head against his shoulder, he nibbled her ear and she closed her eyes in contentment, his hands began to wander and he started to undo the buttons of her blouse revealing a sultry pink camisole, her nipples were erect and straining against the silk, how could he refuse and he bent his head to tease them, as his warm breath came into contact with her nipple Lizzy shuddered and pressed herself harder against him, his erection strained against her bottom so she rotated her hips slowly rubbing herself against him, she could feel him growing harder and his breath quickening. With his free hand Luke unbuttoned her trousers and they slithered down her legs pooling at her feet, she stepped out of them and pushed them aside, standing in her silky French knickers she felt brazen and reached behind her to unbutton and unzip him freeing his massive erection, it nestled between her cheeks moist with the effort of controlling his urge to be inside her. He traced her sex through the silk and could feel how wet she was, this spurred him on and he pushed the panties down her thighs freeing her, he guided his cock between her legs and as she responded by leaning over the kitchen counter he slid into her moving slowly at first, she met him move for move and grabbing her hips he ground himself into her, taking her from behind; as he felt her muscles tighten he knew this was his undoing and as she came he swiftly followed jerking against her as he came deep inside her. He collapsed against her and held her tightly to him savouring the sweet smell of her. God he loved her so much and boy did his body know it, he only had to think of her or look at her and he would feel himself harden, she was his Angel, his miracle and he would protect her for the rest of his life, he would commit murder for her if anyone hurt her or he would die trying.

Chapter 24

They ate together and as Lizzy was clearing away the dishes there was a knock on the door, Luke went to see who it was and came back with Eric one of the doormen, "I have to go out for a while Liz," he told her, "there's been some trouble at one of the houses, usual fighting over a good looking punter, apparently one of the girls is a right mess!" he put on his jacket and came back to kiss her goodbye, "I won't be long I'll deal with the other girl and get the injured one down the local hospital, will you be OK?"

"I'll be fine, Luke, I have some books to look at before tomorrow and it'll be easier to get started if you're not here distracting me!" she told him smiling coyly. With that he slapped her backside and was gone, Eric following. Lizzy spent the next two hours reading the latest anatomy assignment then decided to have a nice soak in the bath while she waited for Luke to return, having pampered herself she chose a pretty pink negligee, put some soft music on the record player poured herself a glass of wine and with the mood set waited for him to arrive. About half an hour later there came a gentle tapping on the door, Lizzy went to the door and asked who was there.

"It's me, Eric," came the reply.

"Hold on a sec," she told him and went to grab her robe, once she had covered herself she answered the door. He came into the flat and looked around at the romantic setting Lizzy had set while waiting for his boss to come home, she was a fine looking woman and had a great body, he could make out her curves beneath the robe she had donned.

"How can I help you?" Lizzy asked him.

"Oh, I've just come to let you know, the trouble is taking a bit longer to sort but Luke won't be too long," Eric informed her.

"Thanks," she replied. "Can I offer you a drink?" she was used to Eric popping in from time to time and he quite often had a cuppa if the club was quiet as Mark the other doorman could cope.

"That would be great, I'm proper parched and it's a cold one tonight, thanks, Lizzy."

She told him to take a seat and went into the kitchen to put the kettle on, as she waited for the kettle to boil she went about taking the pots off the drainer and putting them away, she did not notice Eric enter the kitchen until she turned and he was standing behind her.

"Oh," she said. "You startled me."

Eric did not speak but looked at her and before she could react his hand shot out and was around her throat, she struggled to release his hand and began to feel faint as he squeezed harder, she slapped at him and he released her to grab her wrists, terrified she tried to free herself, but he was too strong for her and he held her fast. Eric managed to grab both her wrists in one of his meaty hands and with his free hand he began tugging at her robe, his hand was groping her through the thin silk and as she opened her mouth to scream his fist connected with her jaw knocking her to the floor, momentarily she lay there dazed. He grabbed the opportunity and slammed on top of her, his weight knocked the breath out of her and as she lay there helpless, unable to move she could feel him unzipping his trousers. As realisation kicked in she knew what he wanted and fought him, kicking out which earned her another punch to the face, as the metallic taste of blood filled her mouth she spat at him showering his face with her blood, he never spoke just looked at her with a demonised look on his face leering down at her as she struggled pitifully to free herself, but he was too heavy and she knew she was defeated.

Lizzy lay there and silently prayed Luke would come soon, Eric had managed to free himself from his trousers and his ugly red cock bounced against her thigh as she wriggled from left to right not giving him any opportunity to touch her with it, frustrated he began punching her about the face and body. Weakened and in pain she lay beneath him and he took his chance as he plunged his cock into her, the pain made her scream out and he stuffed the tea towel she had been holding into her mouth to drown out her screams, as he mercilessly fucked her the pain was like a hot poker tearing at her insides, he grabbed her hair and wrenched it as he pounded into her his face sweating, dripping onto her face and body, for what seemed like an eternity he pounded into her, her cheeks wet with the silent tears that coursed her face. When he came she felt his climax hot and burning inside her, she turned her head and heaved into her hair this incensed him even more and he flipped her over where he slapped her buttocks with such a force it burned, she could feel him growing hard again and prayed for god to help her, he grabbed her hair again and bashed her head onto the cold stone floor.

"Please," she whispered, "someone help me."

Eric heard her and laughed. " No-one is coming you slag, Luke will be ages yet, so it's just you and me for now and I've only just started, bitch," with one swift rip he uncovered the rest of her body and sank his teeth into her shoulder drawing blood, this seemed to spur him on and he kept biting her over and over again, she could feel his cock shuddering on her back but was powerless to do anything, as she wept she knew he would not leave until he had done with her. Her head hurt, her body hurt and her insides were on fire she could feel blood trickling from her and sliding down her thighs, Eric grabbed his cock and was trying to guide it into her but from this position her legs were closed not allowing him entry, then she felt the most horrendous pain slowly her fuddled mind began to comprehend what he was trying to do, he was trying to enter her bottom, horrified she tried to move away from him but in her haste to get away she had raised herself on her knees and this was all he needed, he shoved into her from behind and this time his cock penetrated her backside and the pain seemed to rip her in two, not only had he raped her he was now sodomizing her and she could not stop him. Lizzy had never felt pain like this in her life, her screams muffled as he pushed her head into the floor, then he withdrew and as she caught her breath he plunged his cock in again and the searing pain began again, he did this several times and as he began to quiver with his orgasm he withdrew from her and ejaculated all over her back the warm foul smelling liquid made her retch and as she did he rubbed her face in it all the time chanting, "Dirty bitch, dirty bitch, dirty bitch."

Lizzy felt his weight lift off her but she had no energy and simply lay there on the kitchen floor amongst her own blood, tears and vomit, she heard the taps running as he washed himself but she had nothing left in her to move. He re-boiled the kettle and poured himself a coffee, all the while talking to her, telling her that she had asked for it, his voice was distant and echoed in her muddled mind, he rinsed his cup and placed it on the drainer then he turned to her and bent down, her body flinched expecting more pain but he simply said, "Thanks Lizzy we should do it again sometime" and with that she heard the soft click as he left the flat and closed the door behind him. Lizzy tried to move, but the pain was too much for her and as her body failed her she drifted into blissful unconsciousness lying there on the kitchen floor and this is where Luke and Gerry found her half an hour later.

Chapter 25

Luke had left the flat and driven to the brothel on Winchester road, he parked up and went in, the reception area was a mess and this by the looks of it was where the cat fight had taken place, Eileen greeted him and explained what had happened, she was a good sort and still had some of her looks from her younger years. Eileen had been a tom for most of her life and when Gerry had opened this place she had come to work for him but as the years went by she no longer had the heart for the game and Gerry had made her manager. She was good with the girls and fair, also she never fiddled the books which was a bonus in this game and Gerry trusted her. She had already sent the troublemaker away with her cards and the injured tom had been taken to the hospital for stitches and a general clean up, Luke was a bit pissed off at having his evening ruined for no real reason, but Eric had made it sound like he was needed here so with a shrug he had a quick brew, a catch up with Eileen and was out of there, as he drove home he detoured to the Blue Diamond to catch up with Gerry. They had a scotch and went over the books from the newly acquired bookies on the high street, Luke had a knack for figures and could spot a fiddle a mile off, the former owner had been dipping into the profits for years and the place was as run down as it could get, Gerry being Gerry had the golden touch and Luke knew before too long the bookies would be a right little money earner. With the business dealt with Luke rose to leave and as an afterthought he turned to Gerry and asked, "Do you want to pop round boss, Lizzy has made a cracking trifle and knowing your sweet tooth a bit for supper would go down a right treat!"

"Aye I don't mind if I do and it's always a pleasure to see that gal of yours, I'll follow in my motor then I can head home from yours. Also gives me an excuse to check on the club."

With that Gerry locked the office and they were on their way. They went through the club and although it was still reasonably early, well it was 10 p.m., early for a club, the place was filling up nicely, they chatted a while to Mark on the door.

"Where's Eric?" Luke asked, to which Mark replied:

"Said he didn't feel well so I sent him off home, he did look a bit flushed come to think of it."

Satisfied that all was ticking over well the two men carried on through the club, up the private stairs and Luke unlocked the door shouting to Lizzy that he was home as they entered. The only noise in the front room was the humming of the record player that had finished playing.

"She must have gone to bed," Luke said. "That's unusual she always waits up for me." With a shrug went through to the kitchen and the sight that met him would haunt him for the rest of his life, he stopped so suddenly that Gerry ran into the back of him, but what he saw over Luke's shoulder made his blood run cold, this is how both men found his beautiful angel, she was so still that Luke thought she was dead she didn't appear to be breathing so still was her body not even a sense of her breathing could be seen.

Chapter 26

The usually pristine kitchen was like a murder scene, there were blood splatters up the cupboards and on the floor, in the middle of this lay Lizzy she was on her front and her badly bloodied, bruised body was naked, her clothes lay around her in tatters, an eerie stillness resonated around the kitchen. Momentarily both men stood and stared not quite believing what they were looking at, it was Gerry that sprang into action he shoved Luke aside and knelt down by Lizzy, his shaking hand gently moved her matted hair and felt her neck for a pulse as he touched her she whimpered faintly.

"She's alive, son," Gerry said and turned to look at Luke, he was standing there in the doorway silent tears coursing down his face. "Luke, move, go downstairs and call an ambulance," Gerry urged him but still Luke stood there. "LUKE GO NOW GET HELP!" Gerry shouted, this time Luke focussed on him and turned, running from the flat and down the stairs, he burst into the bar and shouted at the bar staff, anyone really to call an ambulance. When he ran back up to the flat Gerry had covered Lizzy with a blanket and was sitting next to her in her blood and vomit holding her hand and talking to her quietly as one would a child, Luke fell to his knees the other side of her and called her name over and over he chanted her name so quietly he was barely audible, he reached out to touch her and his hand hovered in the air, he didn't know where to touch her she was so badly bruised and the blood, Luke could taste it, the metallic smell seeping into his nose, his hand rested upon her cheek and he gently caressed it, looking up at Gerry. The anguish and fear in his eyes brought tears to Gerry's eyes he had never seen Luke this way, this hard man whom he considered his son looked lost, unable to comprehend that this was his Lizzy. They sat like this, together until a commotion on the stairs brought Mark and two ambulance men into the kitchen, all three stopped dead at the sight that met them.

"What the fuck…" Mark said and looked from Luke to Gerry waiting for them to speak, Gerry shrugged he had no idea what had happened here, but it wasn't good and there would be repercussions of that he was sure. One of the ambulance men placed a hand on Luke's shoulder.

"Come away, son we need to take a look at her," Gerry rose and took hold of Luke bringing him to his feet and steered him away so the men could do their job. They checked her to see if she was breathing and her airways were clear then for any broken bones, satisfied nothing vital appeared to be broken, they conferred with each other in hushed tones and the first one rose; he turned to Gerry, Luke and Mark.

"We need to get her into the ambulance and to hospital, she's in a bad way, we will carry her down between us as we can't get the trolley up here," he turned back to his colleague and for the first time since they arrived Luke spoke.

"I'll carry her." He moved towards her and gently lifted her up into his arms, he cradled her with such a tenderness it moved the men in that room, this was a moment none of them would forget in a hurry. Luke carried her out of the flat, down the stairs and into the club, the place was in silence, no one knew what had happened but they knew it was bad, as he walked through the packed club people parted to make a walkway through for him and the other men that followed. Luke stared straight ahead his thoughts of nothing else than his Angel.

Chapter 27

The ambulance tore through the streets with its lights blazing followed by Gerry and Luke. The ambulance went round to the emergency entrance and Gerry parked up, he led Luke into the reception area and sat him down then he went to speak to the nurse on duty and told her why they were there, she in turn promised she would let them know when she had any news. Gerry thanked her and went back over to sit with Luke, neither man spoke for a while; they just sat there with Lizzy's blood on them deep in thought. Gerry could not for the life of him imagine who would do this to another person let alone Lizzy, she was the kindest, most gentle person he had ever met, everyone loved her, why? Luke startled him when he spoke.

"I will kill whoever did this, Gerry, of that you can be sure, this is the work of an animal, scum of the earth and deserves to be erased from this world, I will hurt him as badly as he has hurt my Lizzy!"

"I know, son, I know," was all Gerry could say because he knew how Luke felt and he himself wanted to commit murder. "I promise you we will find who did this and you can have him." He looked at Luke and nodded, he would find this scum and he would keep his word, no one touches his own and lives to talk about it, God only

76

knew what went on in that flat tonight and how much that poor gal had suffered, but he would pay. The circles they moved in would know by tomorrow that he was looking for information, the problem with the world they lived in people talked, there were no secrets in this life not unless the fear of god was installed in those involved. No one crossed him and his without consequence someone would pay for this.

Chapter 28

Several hours passed and by now Luke was pacing the floor, backwards and forwards he went muttering to himself, finally a doctor in bloodied scrubs came out to see them.

"I'm Dr Stone and I've operated on Lizzy, nothing life threatening but she has been hurt badly."

"Will she be OK?" Luke asked.

"Physically she will mend, she has three broken ribs, countless bite marks, cuts all over her body, I'm afraid she looks a mess as she is covered in bruises, she has a fractured skull. I have sealed the fracture and all looks well there. I am afraid this next part is not pleasant, but I've had to do some extensive stitching both in her vagina and her anus, she was badly raped and sodomised, I'm sorry. But she will heal and she will still be able to have children, but emotionally she will need time, she has been through an ordeal I cannot comprehend nor imagine, I have never seen this amount of injuries done on a woman, she is lucky to be alive, but she's a fighter and she is hanging in there."

As he rose to leave, Luke rose with him and asked, "Can I see her doctor, please?"

The doctor hesitated and then said, "Just for a few minutes, she is sedated and I must reiterate she looks a mess so be prepared, come with me."

Luke followed the doctor down the corridor, up a flight of stairs and onto a ward, at the far end was a private room with its curtains closed; the doctor opened the door and motioned for Luke to follow. As he entered the room he gasped, there lay Lizzy bruised and bandaged, hooked up to drips and oxygen, she looked so small and frail in that hospital bed. His throat constricted and his eyes pricked, he swallowed several times to stop the tears from coming; composing himself he knelt by her bed and gently took her delicate hand in his, he raised it to his lips and held it there, she was warm and soft and he wanted to scoop her up into his arms and hold her, keep her safe because he had failed her, she had been hurt and he wasn't there to protect her. It wasn't until the doctor spoke that he realised he was crying, embarrassed he wiped his face and mumbled, "Sorry," the doctor placed his hand on Luke's arm and smiled.

"She will heal, son, but it will be slow, if you love her as much as it shows then she will be OK. Come back tomorrow, go home, get some sleep and come back in the morning. She will be fine the nurse will sit with her all night, don't worry."

Luke nodded his appreciation, he bent over and kissed Lizzy then he left the room and went back the way he had come to where Gerry was waiting. Gerry hugged him to him and together they left the hospital, "You're coming home with me tonight while I get that flat cleaned up," Luke didn't have the energy to argue, he felt as if the life had been zapped out of him so he got in the car and Gerry drove off. They drove in silence until Gerry pulled into his driveway and cut the engine.

"Who the hell would do something like this?" Luke asked him.

Gerry shook his head and replied, "I don't know, but we will find him, I've already called in a few favours while I was waiting for you, we are already looking and we will find him, son, now come on, let's get you inside."

Hilda greeted them at the door and she pulled Luke into her arms as best she could for she was a petite woman and Luke towered over her, he held onto her and sobbed, she comforted him with gentle words. Once they were all seated in the expansive kitchen, a scotch apiece, Hilda was the first one to speak.

"So what has happened?" she asked, Gerry had rung her and warned her something bad had happened and that he would be bringing Luke back so she should make up a bed. Luke explained what the doctor had said, when he had finished Hilda was crying silently, she gulped down her drink, blew her nose, wiped her eyes and looked up at both men.

"You will find this scum," not a question but a statement and they both nodded at her. "Right then off to bed the pair of you because we have a poorly girl to look after and you two have some serious work to do," With that she got down from the stool and left the room, Gerry reached out and touched Luke's arm.

"Come on, son, try and get some sleep." Luke lay in the dark staring at the ceiling, every time he closed his eyes all he could see was his Angel lying on the kitchen floor beaten and covered in blood. She should be lying in his arms in their bed. Eventually he fell asleep but slept the sleep of the tormented. When the light peeked through the curtains he was relieved to have gotten through the night at all. As he laid there he swore to himself and to the empty room that he would find this sick son of a bitch and he would make him suffer just as his Lizzy had. There would be no mercy for this person, not if he had anything to do with it, with that in the forefront of his mind he rose, washed his face and dressed, moved on by the hatred he had for this man that had ruined his beautiful angel.

Chapter 29

Gerry was already seated at the breakfast bar eating eggs and bacon, Luke took a seat opposite him and Hilda placed another plate of bacon and eggs in front of him and a mug of tea.

"I'm not hungry, Hilda," he told her.

"Just try to eat a bit, you need to keep your strength up," she replied.

Luke took a mouthful and as the taste of smoky bacon filled his mouth he realised he was actually hungry and proceeded to wolf the lot.

"You heard anything yet?" he asked Gerry, who shook his head. "Well if you wouldn't mind giving me a lift to the hospital maybe Lizzy is awake and can tell us what happened," Luke responded.

"I hope so, son," Gerry replied.

Chapter 30

Gerry dropped Luke at the front entrance with a promise of being back in a couple of hours, he wanted to check out the flat to make sure his instructions had been carried out before Luke went back there. He drove to the club, let himself in and made his way up the stairs to the flat, he could hear the radio so assumed the lads were still there, entering the flat he could smell paint, wood and varnish, a pretty potent mixture and wrinkling his nose he made his way through to the kitchen. Paddy and George, brothers by name but complete opposites by looks and nature, Paddy was a little simple but quiet and kind, his brother on the other hand was a typical rogue and renowned for being a ladies' man. But he sure was a good-looking bloke with his mop of red hair and temper to match.

"Boss," they both greeted him. "What do you think?"

Gerry looked around the kitchen which had been transformed, he had ordered it gutted and redone, the boys had done a grand job they had built new cupboards, re decorated and replaced every stick of furniture and kitchen appliances, Gerry did not want anything in this kitchen to remind Lizzy of her ordeal and he was pleased with what he saw the place was fit for a queen.

"You've done me proud, boys, thank you," he told them and reaching into his pocket he handed both lads a hefty wad. "You've well earnt this."

The lads beamed, they had been working all night and were pleased they had done a good job, they liked and respected both Gerry and Luke and were gutted that his wee lass had been attacked, the rumour mongers had started and they knew she had been hurt bad, so doing this had not been a hardship but a pleasure and would go far to keep them in good books. Gerry left them to it and went downstairs into the office behind the bar, he sat at the desk and got on the phone, he rang around to see if anyone had uncovered any news about last night's events but after an hour or so and countless calls he was no nearer to finding out what had happened.

"Well let's hope Lizzy is awake and can tell us who it was," he mumbled to himself.

Chapter 31

Luke had walked back down the same corridor he had walked last night, up the stairs and onto the ward, as he got to the room Lizzy was in he saw a policeman sat outside, they acknowledged each other and he opened the door to walk in. Lizzy was lying in bed and an older woman and man were in the room, the woman was seated next to the bed and the man stood by the window watching the bed. As he entered they both looked in his direction but he was looking at Lizzy and to his relief she was looking back at him, he went to her and kissed her cheek, she raised her hand and gently touched his face, a gesture that touched his heart, she whispered his name but it came out as a croak, her throat was sore from the tube she'd had inserted down her throat during surgery it the night before. Luke looked up to the man and offered his hand by way of greeting.

"I'm Luke," he said, but the man did not return his handshake, he just stared with a hatred burning in his eyes; his stance showed the anger he was struggling to control, finally he spoke.

"So you are the young villain that has taken my daughter and then allowed for her to be attacked," he viciously spat at Luke, stunned Luke did not know what to say and looking at Lizzy he suddenly realised that these were her parents.

"William, please. He didn't cause this." The woman rose as she spoke, she looked to Luke and introduced herself. "I'm Briony, Lizzy's mother and that is William her father, Luke acknowledged her and for a second their eyes met, she could see how much this man was suffering and how much he loved her daughter, she placed a gloved hand on his arm and gestured for him to sit in the seat she had just vacated she then turned to William and said.

"Come now we will leave these two and come back this afternoon."

William leant towards Lizzy and kissed her cheek, "See you later," he said and left the room.

Briony lifted her daughter's hand and gently kissed it "We will be back later, darling," she told her. She turned to Luke and said, "He's angry but he will calm down, she's his little girl and he cannot bear to see her like this." With that she left the room gently closing the door behind her. Luke looked up and Lizzy was watching him, one eye was completely blackened and closed, the swelling evident, she reached for his hand and he held it gently not wanting to hurt her, neither spoke for a while they just looked at each other.

"I'm sorry," she eventually croaked.

Puzzled he questioningly looked at her and asked "What for?"

"For letting this happen," she replied.

"Don't you dare, this was not your fault in any way, don't you ever say that again, ever," he replied. "But, Angel, I have to ask you, do you know who did this?" Lizzy's good eye filled with tears and she nodded at him, Luke reached over and wiped the tears that had fallen on her cheek, "Who, Angel?" he asked, Lizzy turned her head away and her shoulders shook, it broke Luke's heart to see her like this but he didn't dare reach out to her for fear of hurting her so he gently turned her head and asked her again. "Who was it?" Lizzy whispered so softly Luke thought he had misheard her.

"Eric?" he asked frowning. "Is that what you said, Angel?" she nodded and watched his face for a reaction but Luke was so surprised he didn't know what to say, Eric worked for them he was a decent enough bloke, lived with his old mum. Then he thought back to the previous evening when Eric had fetched him to tell him he was needed, but when he had arrived they didn't need him which he had thought odd but shrugged it off, so all the time he was out Eric was up in their flat doing this to his Angel! The anger that was welling within Luke was so powerful he could feel his whole body reacting, he wanted to rip Eric's face off. Lizzy could feel the anger washing over him and she squeezed his hand to get his attention.

"Please, Luke, don't do anything stupid, the police have already been here and they will be keeping tabs on all this, I don't want to lose you, if you do something stupid they'll lock you up."

He dropped his head. "I can't sit by and do nothing, I should have protected you better and I failed," he told her.

"No you didn't, you couldn't have known what would happen," she replied. Luke stayed for a while until Lizzy fell asleep, letting himself out he quietly closed the door behind him and went back to the reception area to meet Gerry.

Chapter 32

Eric had always been a bit odd, 'special' his mother called it. He had never really got on with girls, as a child he would torment them and pull their pigtails, but he loved his old mum, you could say he was very much a mummy's boy. Several years back there had been some trouble with Sally Porter the girl who had worked behind the bar at the Duck and Drake, she had gone to the police accusing Eric of trying to have sex with her, she'd fought him off eventually with a good kick in the balls. Admittedly she had been battered a bit and her clothes were torn but it had been her word against his and she had no alibi whereas Eric's mum had said he was at home with her, he wasn't, but in her eyes Eric would never do anything like that and that Sally was a right one and didn't follow God's word carrying on with men before marriage, she was a whore. Eric's mum was a devout catholic and Eric had been brought up proper, with respect and to live by God's rules, well so his mum thought, Eric was not a nice person, he was at work and with his colleagues, a bit of a jack the lad was the impression he gave, but he was well known within the tom world, he had gotten rough with many girls, violence was what turned him on. He had gone home from the club last night, bathed, thrown his clothes in the wash basket and gone out, so when the police had arrived this morning he had still not returned home, they questioned his mum but she didn't know where he was and if truth be known she wouldn't have told them anyway, her Eric was a good boy. Eric was in fact holed up with a tom on the Leyland estate, as long as he kept her in drugs she wouldn't care or notice who was there, so he was sure he was safe for now, he knew he had gone too far this time and of all people it was Luke Barton's bit he had done over, she had deserved it, though, fluttering her eyelashes at him and flirting around him, she was like all the rest, a whore and needed to be treated as such. The truth of it was, though, Lizzy had never been anything but kind to Eric, this was all in his head, God had taught him all about women, look at Eve, he considered women the scum of the earth, dirty and evil doing the devil's work and as such they deserved to be treated anyway he saw fit. Although he knew he had gone a bit far he honestly thought he had done Luke a favour by showing him what a dirty whore she was. It never occurred to him that he had sealed his own fate, he just thought if he laid low for a few days the police would lose interest and then he could go back home.

Chapter 33

Gerry was waiting for Luke out in the carpark, pleased that the flat was all but finished apart from new locks and chains on the two main doors, as Luke approached the car Gerry could see the look on his face and he wasn't happy by any means. Luke climbed into the car turned to Gerry and said, "It was Eric."

Gerry looked at him for a moment and replied. "Eric that works the door?"

Seething, Luke replied, "Yep, that's the bastard."

"Oh God," was all Gerry could think of – "Eric? But why? "OK, let's get to the office and I'll get him picked up, we'll try his mum's see if he's there or if she knows where he is."

With that Gerry started the car and drove off.

Chapter 34

On the other side of town Eric was also the topic of conversation at the local nick. Inspector Hastings was having a cuppa in the canteen with his sergeant, Joe Knowles, they had been friends for over twenty years and they had seen some things in their time but that was usually with the toms, not a middle class girl at home being attacked as viciously as Lizzy had been. "There's going to be ructions, Joe, you know it and I know it, she's the girlfriend of a well-known face for God's sake and those villains protect their own, this is not going to end well, if they get to him first then heaven help him. To be honest, Joe, he deserves everything he gets after what he did to her," the two men sighed and knew this case would be closed very soon as the perp would no longer be around.

Chapter 35

Lizzy woke and was quite relieved to find she was alone, she hurt a lot and she was ashamed, the doctor had been to see her earlier and had told her what had been done to her, Luke will never want me now she thought not after what he did to me, how could he I'm dirty now. Her tears fell silently, she wanted Luke to love her like he used to, but she was different she wasn't the woman she had been yesterday, the thought of him touching her intimately scared her to death and if they couldn't make love why would he stay? She knew Luke would find Eric and kill him and as much as she didn't want him to get into trouble she secretly wanted him to kill Eric, to erase him from their lives because while he lived she was scared. She knew she looked a state and her insides burned with a pain so excruciating she didn't think the pain would ever go so severe it was, but she was alive, the doctor had told her she would heal and thank God she could still some day have children; he had not taken that away from her. She had been surprised to see her parents but the police had informed them, she knew they wanted her to come back home with them, but if she did she would lose Luke, no she couldn't do that, they wanted her to go home to recoup but once there they would never let her go or let Luke see her, she would speak to Gerry and see if she could go to his, to Hilda, she would help her mend and Luke could stay if he wanted to, more confident now she had made a decision she drifted back off to sleep, sleep was a reprieve from the pain both in her body and her heart.

Chapter 36

Gerry had sent a couple of his lads around to Eric's house and they had been sent away with a flea in their ears by his mum, so now Gerry had people searching all the places they thought he may frequent but their searching had been to no avail for the moment.

Luke was pacing the office like a caged lion, "Where the fuck is he?" he seethed at Gerry. "This is doing my head in, he could be anywhere!"

Gerry sighed, he was just as frustrated that he had disappeared, but what more could he do; no stone was being left unturned. "He'll show up eventually, no one can hide forever, Luke."

Luke put on his jacket and told Gerry he was off to the hospital to see Lizzy then he would be back to take care of some work,

"Go home after the hospital, Luke," Gerry told him "You're in no fit state to be at work the mood you are in, as soon as I hear anything I'll let you know, OK?" Luke nodded and left the office. He arrived at the hospital around 5 p.m. just as Lizzy's parents were leaving, they acknowledged each other and then they were gone.

"How you feeling, Angel?" He asked Lizzy.

"I'm in a lot of pain, but they keep doping me up so I am sleeping a lot, but then if I sleep I don't have to remember for a while," she replied.

Luke was so thrilled that she was going to be OK but also so sorry that he had not been there to stop this from happening.

"I am so sorry, Angel, I should have been there to look after you, I've failed the one person I love more than anything," Luke told her and when he looked at her he had tears in his eyes that choked her and tugged at her heart.

"You are not to blame for this and I don't blame you at all, you're here now that's what counts. I have been so scared that you wouldn't want me anymore as I'm soiled and dirty," she replied her voice quivering with emotion.

He reached for her hand and kissed her fingers, his tears hot on her skin, she pulled him to her and they lay together on the hospital bed, his arms protectively around her holding her tight and safe in his embrace, no words were needed they knew they would get through this one way or another so strong was their love for each other. They lay like this for a long time and eventually fell sleep together each with their own thoughts, his mentally going through what he would do to Eric when they found him and he would make that bastard pay for this, her with her wishes that she would again want a relationship with Luke because at the moment any form of intimacy scared her to death, so ferocious had the attack on her been that she was scared he would hurt her or she would relive the memories every time they made love. Luke started as he heard the door open and protectively shielded Lizzy but it was the nurse coming to check on her and do her observations, she smiled at them and carried on with her duties, as she was checking Lizzy's temperature she awoke and sighed peacefully as she felt the warmth of

Luke's body against hers. When the nurse had gone she whispered to him.

"Thank you for staying with me," Luke looked at her beaten face and winced as she gasped through pain as she tried to turn to face him, he kissed her nose, her forehead, her good eye and then he looked at her swollen lips and gently kissed them. Lizzy parted her lips slightly and tried to kiss him back but that small act was so painful that he placed a finger on her lips and nodded that he understood.

"There will be time for that when you're better," he told her and smiled, though he was worried about being intimate with her, what if he hurt her, what if mentally she couldn't bear him inside her? We will take it one step at a time he told himself. Just as Luke was getting ready to leave, Gerry arrived with a huge bunch of flowers.

"How's my favourite gal doing?" He asked Lizzy.

"Better," she replied, he stayed for a few minutes and then waited outside for Luke to say his goodbyes.

"I'll be back in the morning, Angel, if you need me then get the nurse to ring and I'll be straight back," He kissed her gently and then left closing the door behind him. Gerry and Luke walked down the corridor and out into the carpark; there, Gerry stopped him.

"We've got him, son, he was hiding out at a tom's place on the Leyland estate, he's at the scrap yard on the Morrel road a couple of the lads are holding him there,"

Luke looked at Gerry and for a moment said nothing then he said, "What are we waiting for then, let's teach this scum a lesson in etiquette."

They went in Gerry's car and soon arrived at the locked gates of the scrapyard, the two Alsatian guard dogs growled menacingly and bared their teeth, Andy came out of the porta cabin and called the dogs to him, he was the only one who had any control over these dogs, he'd had them since pups and had bought them up to protect, they loved him that was clear but hated everyone else, once he had chained them he unlocked and opened the heavy gates. Gerry drove in and Luke jumped out of the passenger seat.

"Where is he?" he asked Andy.

"In there," Andy pointed at the porta cabin, Luke was up the steps and in the porta cabin before Gerry had the chance to get out of the car, he hastily leapt out and went straight up the stairs into the office area. Eric had obviously taken a beating from Paddy and George who stood either side of him; he was tied to a chair with his head hung. When Gerry entered the room he looked up and seeing Luke he smiled at him. Luke flew at him but Gerry held him back.

"Wait, son, he needs to suffer for what he's done," he said and suffer Eric did.

Chapter 37

Having composed Luke for the minute Gerry stood in front of Eric, looked him up and down and then with a conceptual loathing asked him, "Why Eric? Why did you do that to Lizzy?" to which Eric responded but looking at Luke.

"I did you a favour, man, she's like all the rest, a whore who needed showing her place, women are beneath us, look at what Eve did to Adam, temptresses the lot of them and if you let them get above themselves they will be the doing of us all." For a moment all four men just stared at him, he was as mad as a box of spanners! The silence was broken by the resonating sound of Luke's fist connecting with Eric's face, his neck jerked backwards and his nose exploded, blood splattering over Paddy and George who never batted an eye just watched Eric as he sneered at Luke.

"Is that the best you've got, call yourself a hard man!"

Luke could control his temper no longer, all he could see was his beloved Lizzy lying in the kitchen of their flat like a broken doll, bleeding and hurt so badly, the thoughts in his head incensed him further and with fists clenched he looked across at Gerry who nodded his head and the beating began. After several minutes Luke stood back breathing heavily, Eric's face was unrecognisable it was a mass of flapping skin, blood and bones sticking out, he definitely wasn't sneering anymore and had passed out but still Luke was not satisfied.

"Get a bucket of cold water," he told Paddy.

Gerry touched his arm and guided Luke to a chair where he pushed him down, he opened the drawer of the filing cabinet and produced a bottle of scotch and four tumblers; he then poured each man a dram and handed it to them.

"Throw the water over him, Paddy. I want him conscious before I finish him off," Luke instructed.

Gerry lit a fag and handed it to Luke who rarely smoked but dragged long and hard on it, Eric stirred and Paddy threw more water over him. Eric gained consciousness and the four men watched him as they finished their drinks and smoked their fags. Luke rose and went to the toolbox by the door he rummaged around and came back with a pair of bolt croppers, standing above Eric he began work on his fingers, cutting them off one by one, slowly and methodically all the while talking to him in a low voice explaining that with no fingers he could not touch another woman, when finished he stood back to admire his handiwork.

"More water, Paddy," he said. "Now Eric, my old China, I'm going to do one last thing before you die, I'm going to make sure that you never have another chance or the ability to hurt women ever again, but then you'll be dead, but if it's the afterlife you believe in then well, it's not going to too enjoyable for you is it, mate?" Turning to George he instructed him to pull down Eric's trousers, George blanched as he realised exactly what Luke was going to do, but he did as he was told and soon Eric was sitting there with his glory on show laying flaccidly in his groin, he had begun to whimper now as he anticipated what was to come, he knew he was done for from this life, but not this, please God, he had done all of God's good work, look at all the women he had taught a lesson to and there had been a lot. Luke stepped forward and it was he that was sneering now, so incensed was he, all he could think about was his Angel, he positioned the croppers and with one good chop Eric's penis lay at his feet but it was the howl of pain that had the men's attention, like a wounded animal or worse, nothing they had ever heard, this was the last thing Eric saw before the blood pumped from him and he took his last breath, breaking the stunned silence Luke spoke.

"Boys I want his head off and bagged then dumped on his mother's doorstep, fucking religious whackos, everyone will see this example and if ever a man on our manner takes it upon himself to do similar to a woman then this will be their punishment, understand?"

Both men nodded.

"Dump the rest of him; I don't care where, just don't let it ever be found." He turned to Gerry and said, "A toast I think to a job well done!"

Now the deed had been done the atmosphere warmed and for a moment they stood and enjoyed the heat of the scotch as it hit the back of their throats and left a warm trail down. Gerry thanked the lads and turned to Luke.

"For starters you need to clean down you're covered in blood, last thing we need is the law sniffing about, the evidence needs getting rid of, we'll go back to your place and in through the fire escape that way no one will see us, wait here," with that he went to his car and came back with jeans and a shirt. "Get changed," he told Luke. "Lads burn his clothes in the furnace and sort this room." They both nodded and looking at each other knew that wasn't the only thing they were going to be burning tonight, though the rest would need to be in smaller pieces – easily remedied, looking at each other they knew the chainsaw would be needed to chop this disgusting excuse of a main into burnable pieces. With Luke changed he began to follow Gerry out to the car and turned.

"Thanks, Paddy and you George, there'll be a bonus in it for you, but just one more thing. I want everyone to know how he died, not who or where, just that you heard what happened to him, OK?"

"Course, boss," they both said and they would keep this evening to themselves, grasses they were not and the bloke deserved it by all accounts, they'd seen the carnage when they got to that flat that night.

"Thanks, lads," Luke said and with that he was gone. Paddy and George chatted while they worked, finally having dealt with Eric, burnt Luke's and their clothes – luckily they had come prepared, but then this was not the first killing they had seen or aided in so they knew the drill – lastly they had not just cleaned the room but removed the whole porta cabin, handy having a scrap yard. All done they said goodbye to Andy and were on their way.

"Last orders at the local?" George said.

"Aye why not," George replied and off they went with a spring in their step at a good night's work well done, off to begin the spread of their tale, which, come the morning, would be common knowledge around the manor.

Luke sat in the passenger seat as Gerry drove him home, he felt satisfied and pleased that he had rid the world of a sadistic bastard but the worst thing was the ease he had inflicted such horrendous punishment out on another human being. He had always been fair but would fight those that had wronged him and his, he couldn't have let this one go this was his Lizzy and he loved her so much it hurt him to see her broken. For that Eric had to pay, his angel may never be the same again and for that he could never forgive, each time he closed his eyes he could imagine what she must have gone through and it broke his heart so yes, he was justified in what he had done to Eric and he would do it again if needed for his Lizzy. He didn't feel proud about inflicting this kind of punishment on another, he felt assured knowing the man that had done this to her would never hurt anyone or her ever again. That was his justification and god help anyone who did not heed to that warning.

Chapter 38

At first light Eric's mum opened her front door to retrieve the milk and found a black bag on the doorstep next to her milk, tutting she opened it and her scream could be heard all the way down the street, although nearly unidentifiable she at once knew this was the head of her beloved son, a son she had unwittingly turned into a monster with her preaching. Soon anyone who was anyone knew of the punishment that had been dished out on this young man, but there was no sympathy for him due to the horrendous act he had carried out on an innocent young woman, the police arrived to take away the head but there was no evidence for them to follow, the rumours were rife, but deep down they all knew who had done this deed and many believed Eric had got what was coming to him and not a minute too soon.

Chapter 40

The local police had no evidence they knew who may be to blame but without any supporting evidence the rest was just hearsay. The Super was breathing down his inspector's neck to make an arrest and set an example to the local villains that this sort of revenge killing would not go unpunished on his manor, he ordered an arrest warrant for Luke to be brought in. Luke was at home when Mark the doorman knocked on the door, behind him stood two constables who arrested him and took him to the local nick. Mark contacted Gerry who in turn sent his brief to get Luke out; he also contacted Inspector Briggs who was on the payroll and told him to earn his money and help get Luke out. For three hours Luke answered their questions, but it was all a futile effort as they all knew there was no evidence to place Luke with Eric and his alibi checked out, so eventually they let him go with a warning not to go too far.

Chapter 41

Christmas came and went, but there was no call for celebration with Lizzy in the hospital and the shock of the events that had occurred. Luke's birthday came and went also with no celebration but he was not bothered, he was just glad his Angel was on the mend and the filth that had done this to her was gone, never to return, such was the punishment exacted on him and well deserved.

Chapter 42

Over the next couple of weeks Lizzy continued to heal and eventually she was allowed home, Luke arrived to fetch her, much to her father's dismay as he was confident she would come home with them and then he could work on keeping her and Luke apart but Lizzy would not hear of this, she had spoken to both Gerry and Hilda and they were more than happy for her to convalesce at his mansion so having packed up the few things she had they were on their way. It was a relatively short distance to Gerry's place and when they arrived Hilda was waiting on the doorstep as Luke made his way up the long driveway, he pulled up outside and ran around to assist Lizzy out of the passenger seat, Hilda fussed and led them into the kitchen where she insisted Lizzy sit down while she made a pot of tea. She set the pot on the table with a plate of homemade fruitcake and poured the tea. "I've made up a lovely room for you Liz," she told her. "It has a lovely view of the garden and the fields beyond."

"Thank you, you are sure it is OK for me to stay?" Lizzy replied.

"Of course it is. Heavens above Lord knows you need looking after. Look how thin you've become and so pale, a couple of weeks with my cooking and some rest will see you right as rain," Hilda told her. After they had drunk their tea, Hilda rose and offered to show them which room she had made up for Lizzy, they followed her up the stairs and along the landing to the far end, Hilda opened the door and Lizzy stepped inside closely followed by Luke who was carrying her bags.

"Oh, Hilda, it's a lovely room so light and airy," Lizzy turned and told her, she reached for the older woman's hand and squeezed it, her eyes filling with tears at how kind everyone was being to her.

"Liz, you can stay as long as you like, darling, we are very happy to have you, both of you," Hilda replied. With that she disappeared back downstairs and left the two of them alone. Luke put Lizzy's bags down and gently wrapped his arms around her holding her tightly to him, they stood there for a while absorbed in each other in the sheer tenderness that one felt for the other, and Lizzy was the first to speak.

"I might have a lie down," she told Luke, "I feel exhausted, yet I've done nothing for weeks!" Luke kissed her gently and then left her to sleep; he went back downstairs and found Hilda in the kitchen preparing vegetables.

"I'll not be long, I'm just popping out to do some jobs and Lizzy is having a lay down," he told her.

Chapter 43

Over the next couple of weeks Lizzy did in fact rest as Hilda would not hear of her doing anything, she fed her up and pampered to her as if she was her own, clucking around her like an old mother hen, Lizzy started to fill out and her face looked less gaunt the bruises had healed and her face began to resemble the beautiful woman she had developed into. Luke stayed with her at night and he just held her, he was scared to touch her in case he scared her or hurt her and for the moment Lizzy was happy and felt safe wrapped in his arms, they didn't discuss sex as Lizzy still felt ashamed and the thought petrified her, but she knew she must find a way to broach the subject. One late afternoon just as spring was showing its face, Lizzy sat alone in the drawing room next to the window admiring the colours appearing in the garden and her thoughts began to wander. Luke was always not far from her mind, but she was worried, the police just didn't seem to want to stop harassing him over Eric's death, but so far they had managed to find nothing to hold him on, thank God she mused. Her thoughts turned to the evening she had planned, she loved Luke and she missed their closeness, missed the way he made her feel when he touched her intimately, she felt a fluttering in her belly just thinking of the way he brought her to orgasm time and time again, but she was nervous, too, what if she couldn't bear him to touch her, she wanted him to so surely that was a good sign? Sighing she decided not to dwell on it, Hilda had helped her cook a lovely meal for Luke, Gerry would be out and Hilda was visiting with a friend and going bingo for the evening so they would have the house to themselves, she tingled with anticipation rose from the chair and made her way upstairs to get changed. She chose a lovely flowing skirt and blouse for the evening and sat at the mirror to brush her hair, she styled it into a French plait that hung down her back, satisfied she took one last look and got up to go downstairs. As she rose a wave of giddiness and nausea overcame her and she sank back into the chair breathing heavily as she overcame the feelings. "I must have not eaten enough today," she murmured to herself. After a moment and feeling better she got up and went downstairs to wait for Luke.

Chapter 44

The evening went well, they chatted, enjoyed a lovely meal that Hilda had prepared for them and washed it down with a nice bottle of wine. Lizzy rose to make them some coffee and tidied away the dinner pots.

"You feeling OK, Angel?" Luke asked her.

"Yes I am, although I felt a little dizzy earlier but I hadn't really eaten, I feel fine now," she replied.

They drank their coffee and then made their way upstairs, once in the bedroom Luke nervously hung around within the doorway.

"Are you not coming in?" Lizzy asked him.

"I wasn't sure what you would like me to do," Luke responded.

Lizzy went to him, pulled him into the room and closed the door, they stood in front of each other looking into each other's eyes then Luke bent his head and tenderly kissed her lips, she opened her mouth to allow him to explore it with his tongue, their kiss developed into a passionate coupling of their mouths and tongues, when Lizzy pulled away her face was flushed and her lips were full and swollen from their passion. She stepped back and began to unbutton her blouse revealing her erect nipples which were straining for release against the silky material of her camisole, next she unzipped her skirt and let it fall to the floor, she raised her eyes to meet his and although his erection was straining against his jeans he felt nervous, afraid to touch her, she took his hand and gently led him over to the bed where she unbuttoned his shirt and tossed it onto the chair, next she reached for his jeans, her hand brushing his erection eliciting a moan from him, he steadied her hand and whispered, "Are you sure Angel?" In response she kissed him and proceeded to free his erection sliding his trousers down his legs, he stepped out of them and took her into his arms, he gently laid her onto the bed and knelt next to her, caressing her breasts through the thin material; she gasped and closed her eyes. He freed her breasts from the silk and taking a nipple into his mouth he slowly circled it with his tongue, sucking gently then harder as his erection quivered between them, he was so turned on by the thought of being with her in an intimate way that he hoped he could manage to wait and not come there and then. Lizzy moaned beneath him all her fear gone with the passion he created in her whole body, his hands explored her body finding the familiar curves, he moved between her legs and kissed her stomach, her thighs and her soft mound through the silk of her knickers then her lowered the silk covering her sex, with his tongue he gently lapped at her swollen bud, she raised her hips to meet him and gasped at the warmth of his breath on her most intimate parts, spurred on by her reaction he inserted a finger into her, she was so wet and ready for him but he didn't want to rush this, he was conscious of the trauma she had been through and wanted to take her as gently as he could. He sucked, licked and fingered her with a tenderness that started to drive her wild, she tried to reach for him, but he pushed her hands away feeling her clenching and so close, he sucked harder and inserted two fingers building a rhythm, her hips rose and fell meeting his mouth and fingers.

"Please," she gasped and her body jerked releasing her orgasm, it racked through her body leaving her breathless and flushed. As her muscles began to relax she pulled him on top of her and wriggled until she could feel the point of his cock at her opening, looking at each other she nodded and he slowly entered her, sliding in with ease from her wetness, he moved slow and gentle, she arched up to meet his gentle thrusts until he could cope no more and began to thrust into her deeper and deeper, Lizzy clung to him digging her nails into his back but Luke felt no pain, just the pleasure of his climax building with hers, her muscles began to contract as she came around his cock which needed no more encouragement and with a loud groan he joined her and together their bodies jerked with the force of the passion like an electric current running through them. Luke rolled to one side pulling her with him and wrapping his arms around her, neither spoke as they strove to catch their breath, Lizzy snuggled deeper into him and sighed, sated they lay like this for a while as their hearts returned to a slow beat. Lizzy's breathing becoming more settled as she began to doze in the safety of his arms, the arms of the man she loved beyond all else, Luke moved and pulled the covers over them, together they drifted into a contented sleep, wrapped around each other as lovers should.

Chapter 45

Over the weeks everything had quietened down but the police were still poking around asking questions, Gerry had been told by his people on the payroll within the force that the Super was after making an example of the vicious murder of Eric, he wanted to show the criminal fraternity that this sort of revenge killing would not be tolerated and someone would answer for this. Gerry feared that Luke would be that example and he began to formulate a plan.

Chapter 46

Luke awoke to the birds singing and the early morning sun shining through the curtains, Lizzy stirred beside him and for a while he lay there, watching her, content in the knowledge that they had come through this terrible mess and found their way out the other end, together. Lizzy opened her eyes and smiled at him as he lay there looking down on her. He leant down and kissed her full lips, she looked so beautiful lying there beneath him with her hair all mussed with sleep. She returned his kiss and pulled him to her, kissing him more urgently as the familiar stirrings of desire filled her. He caressed her body and then taking her nipple into his mouth he sucked, arching her back she reached down and finding his hard cock began moving her hand up and down, he groaned as he began to near his own climax, she smiled shyly relishing the effect she knew she had on him and then manoeuvred him onto his back, she sat astride him and slowly rubbed herself along his shaft, she was wet for him and she slid along it easily, gently she pushed him into her and gasped at the intensity of her feelings, she rode him and he grasped her hips pushing himself deeper into her, he could feel her quivering and knew she was close, with one swift movement he rolled her over and thrust deeper into her, he lost all sense of everything as his orgasm released and he shot his seed deep inside her; she followed him with her own orgasm clenching around him, he kissed her tenderly and whispered, "I love you so much Lizzy Fenwick, will you marry me?"

Lizzy smiled and looked up at him, "Yes," she said and he hugged her to him, feeling like the luckiest man alive.

Chapter 47

That evening as Hilda, Gerry, Lizzy and Luke sat down to dinner the conversation flowed with work and general chit chat then Gerry became serious and spoke to them all.

"Luke, we have a problem with that damned Super at the nick, he is planning on arresting you for this Eric business."

Lizzy gasped, she could not bear to think of him locked away from her, Luke took her hand and squeezed it reassuringly, Gerry continued.

"I've spoken to some contacts and I think the best thing for us to do is to get you away for a while, just until the heat dies down and I can work on the law, I have a couple of people working on the Commissioner, it seems he has tendencies for little boys, but I need proof, with that I can work on him dismissing the case but I need a bit more time."

To which Luke responded, "I can't leave Lizzy, I won't leave her!"

Lizzy was quiet for a moment and then she spoke. "Luke I think Gerry is right, I will be fine here with Hilda and it's only for a few weeks, isn't it Gerry?"

"Aye that's all, gal," Gerry replied.

They spent the next hour or so going over Gerry's plans, he had arranged for Luke to go to Ireland to his hometown of Donegal, he would go by boat and hide up for a while until arrangements had been made this end. He would leave in the next few days. With the situation sorted for now they chatted a while longer then Gerry rose to leave.

"I've some work stuff to sort out but I'll be back later," he told Hilda.

"More like that little red head you've got stashed in a flat to sort out," Hilda retorted smiling.

"I don't know what you mean," Gerry cheekily retorted and left.

Hilda set about sorting the dinner dishes while Luke and Lizzy went off to the parlour to talk about Luke's coming travel plans, she washed the pots and smiling she mulled over the evening's conversation, she did so wish Gerry would find himself a nice woman to settle down with but he was happy and that made her happy, she mused over how Lizzy would cope without Luke, but it wouldn't be for long and she would look after Lizzy. With the pots done and away she poured herself a good measure of scotch and sat down to think of what lay ahead for them all.

Chapter 48

The morning of Luke leaving arrived, Lizzy helped him pack a bag and they sat together on the bed holding each other, she cried and he held her tighter, when her sobs had ceased he pulled her onto his lap.

"Angel, I will be back before you know it I promise and you will be fine here, Hilda will make sure of it," she looked at him and held his face in her hands. "When I get back I am going to buy you the best engagement ring I can find and we will tell everyone that we are to be wed," he continued.

Her eyes red from crying, she said to him, "You will keep in touch when you can?"

"Of course I will," he told her. "Wild horses wouldn't stop me and I will be back real soon, darling."

They held each other for a while longer and then together they went downstairs to Gerry who was waiting to take Luke to the docks where they had a boat waiting. At the front door he hugged Lizzy to him and tenderly kissed her, she watched as they drove away and Hilda closed the door.

"Come on, lass, let's get you a cup of tea," she said and led Lizzy into the kitchen.

As she busied herself about the kitchen Lizzy pondered on how much she would miss Luke, he was her rock and just knowing he wouldn't be coming back tonight made her sad, but it was better than him being locked in a prison for years. Hilda returned to the table with a pot of tea and some biscuits freshly baked that morning, she poured them both a cup and handed one to Lizzy.

"It will all work itself out, darling," she told Lizzy, "Gerry will not let either of you down, you're both like family to him and he will sort this out as soon as he can."

Lizzy smiled at her and reached for a biscuit, as she lifted it to her mouth an overwhelming nausea washed over her, she ran from the room and just made it to the bathroom before she threw up, Hilda had followed her and as she heaved Hilda held her hair out of her face and rubbed her back, after a few minutes the sickness passed and she rinsed her mouth before sitting on the edge of the bath as she composed herself. Lizzy looked at Hilda and she could see the question on Hilda's face.

"I don't know, Hilda, I've felt sick most mornings for a couple of weeks now. I'm scared, what if I am having a baby?"

Hilda took her in her arms as she began to sob, both women aware that this could be a disaster, whose baby would it be? When Lizzy had calmed Hilda helped her back into the kitchen and sat her down,

"We need to know, Liz, I've a friend who is a midwife I'll give her a shout and get her to come have a look at you, OK?" Lizzy nodded and Hilda went out the back door to look for the gardener's son to go find Nancy Jones and bring her there. An hour later he returned with a flustered looking Nancy in tow.

"What's the hurry, Hilda?" she demanded, "I'm a busy woman, you old goat, not here for your beck and call I'll have thee know!"

"Stop your whinging, woman I need you to look at Lizzy, that poor wee lass I told you about, we need to know if she's with child, can you see?"

Nancy had indeed heard about Lizzy the gossip had been rife for weeks but she knew the truth from her dear friend Hilda whom she had known for many a year. The two women went upstairs to Lizzy's room.

Nancy examined her and asked her, "How long have you felt like this, hen?"

"A few weeks," Lizzy replied, "Am I having a baby?" she asked Nancy.

Nancy nodded and in that instant the bottom fell out of Lizzy's world, she couldn't have a baby she didn't know whose it was, what if it was Eric's? Nancy knew this was not a happy occasion under the circumstances.

"I would say about roughly four months gone," she told them both, knowing that this would indeed coincide with the rape give or take a week or so. Hilda led Nancy back downstairs and offered her a cuppa, the two women talked of the situation and then Nancy was on her way with the promise of secrecy. Hilda went back upstairs and found Lizzy huddled in a chair staring out of the window.

As Hilda entered she turned to her and said, "What am I going to do?" Hilda went to her and wrapped her in her arms. Together they stayed this way for a while until Hilda spoke.

"Do you think it may be Eric's?"

"I don't know, Hilda, it could be Eric's or Luke's, I can't have it as I can't be sure which one." The two women talked about it for a while and then Hilda left

Lizzy to rest. She went downstairs and poured herself a little snifter, medicinal purposes of course.

Chapter 49

Lizzy had never felt so alone in her life, she was thankful Luke was not there, how would she explain this to him, how would he feel? She didn't even know how she felt, there was another human being growing inside of her, but she didn't want it there, not under these circumstances. For a long time Lizzy thought about the situation and slowly as the shock wore off she made plans. She couldn't get rid of it, not only was it not done but she couldn't kill a baby; it wasn't the baby's fault, though God only knew how it could have survived after what Eric had done to her – but it had. That fateful night she and Luke had made love several times, but then there had been the vicious attack by Eric, whose baby was it? So many questions and no answers, Lizzy finally knew what she would do; as day wore into evening she stayed in her room. Hilda brought her sandwiches up and Lizzy ate a little but felt too nauseated to eat any more and eventually she drifted off into a tormented sleep, the night of the attack bringing on nightmares she had stopped having. After a restless night where the demons would not go, Lizzy woke and knew what she would do, she must disappear until the baby had been born but where would she go, she had a little money, but not enough to find nice lodgings, today was Thursday, Hilda's bingo night she would go then.

Chapter 50

Hilda checked in on Lizzy before she left, again asking her if she wanted her to stay with her, Lizzy assured her she would be fine so off Hilda went. As soon as the coast was clear Lizzy packed a bag and then rang Shelley to come fetch her, a little after seven Shelley arrived in a taxi, Lizzy picked up her bag and left her comfort zone. They rode in silence into London and deep into the East End slums, Lizzy instructed the taxi to stop and both women alighted, Shelley paid the driver and he drove off glancing back at the two women standing on the corner of one of the roughest areas, he shrugged and went on his way looking for his next fare before telling himself he would do one more and then go home to his missus whom he knew would be waiting for him with a nice hot meal, it had been a long day. Lizzy and Shelley wandered around looking for lodgings, just when it seemed to be an impossible task they came upon a rundown terrace that had a sign in the window, top floor room for rent. Lizzy knocked on the battered front door and waited, an old woman with curlers in her remaining hair eventually answered the door, she looked the two women up and down and asked them "What di yer want?"

"The room," Lizzy stuttered, "Is it still available?" The old woman eyed them suspiciously.

"Who wants ta know?" she asked her.

"I would like to rent it for a little while please," Lizzy replied.

"It's two bob a week," she replied, smiling and revealing two brown teeth the only ones left in her mouth.

"I'll take it," Lizzy told her.

"That'll be up front then, missus," the old lady told them. Lizzy fumbled around in her bag and handed the money to the old woman who opened the door wider and ushered them in. "Wait 'ere," she told them and disappeared through a door on the left. She returned with a key and beckoned for them to follow her up the stairs; they followed her up three flights and came upon a door at the top.

"Best room in't house," the old women grinned at them. She unlocked the door and in the dark came a scurrying from within, a single bulb hung from the ceiling and as the old woman flicked the switch the dull light lit the room, there was a bed, a chair, a wash basin, a table and a dresser of some sort, the room seemed clean enough but there was no carpet on the floor and the room felt cold, the window was covered by a flimsy net which allowed the light from the street to filter in brightening the room slightly more. The old woman pressed the key into Lizzy's hand and turned to go back down. As an afterthought she turned and told Lizzy the shared bathroom was on the second floor and then she disappeared down the dimly lit staircase. Lizzy closed the door put her bag on the floor and looked at Shelley. As the tears fell, Shelley held her tightly until Lizzy's sobs had subsided.

"Lizzy what is this all about?" she asked her.

"It's all such a mess Shelley," Lizzy sobbed.

The room was cold and Shelley could not bear the thought of her dearest friend being here on her own, there were no covers on the stained mattress, but there was a small wood burner in the corner, an old kettle on the top, just then a knock came on the door and Shelley opened it to find a young, dirty faced urchin standing there his arms full of wood.

"The missus sent me up with this for the burner," he said. He dropped it at Shelley's feet, turned on his heel and was gone back down the stairs as silently as he had arrived. Shelley looked around her and knew she would have to take charge as her friend Lizzy was just standing there absently looking into space.

"Liz, you get a fire going and I'll be back shortly," Lizzy nodded and Shelley left her to start a fire. Leaving the house, Shelley walked to a busier area and hailed a taxi; she would go home and grab some supplies. Her parents were away for the next couple of days, so she would not have to answer any questions.

Chapter 51

Lizzy looked around the room and taking off her coat she rolled up her sleeves and went about building a fire with the wood and scraps of paper she found under the bed, soon she had a fire going adding instant warmth to the room, she went down to the second floor and washed the kettle out then filled it with water, the bathroom was filthy and stank of urine, so treading carefully she made her way back up to the room and placed the kettle on the burner, she looked around her and with a sigh set about looking around to see what she could find. In the dresser she found a couple of plates, two mugs, some utensils, various cooking materials, some clothes and a couple of tea towels, left by the previous tenant she mused, once the water had boiled she filled the small basin and began wiping all the surfaces down, once finished she stood back and looked at her handiwork.

"This place won't be so bad," she murmured, already with the burner lit and now the place looking cleaner it had potential. She could hear banging and cursing and went to the door; she opened it and saw Shelley making her way back up the stairs laden down with bags. Shelley all but fell into the room and deposited her stash on the bed.

"Blimey, that took some carrying," she said, she turned and looked at Lizzy and then both women burst out laughing, they laughed so hard the tears were pouring down their faces, eventually they managed to compose themselves and it was Shelley who managed to speak. "First off Liz let's have a cup of tea and then we will sort this place out, OK?" Lizzy nodded and went back downstairs to fill the kettle. They enjoyed a cup of tea and some sandwiches that Shelley had brought with her in one of the many bundles she had fallen into the room carrying. Next, between them they turned the mattress, which looked slightly better on the other side, Shelley covered it with a thick blanket then made the bed up with the bedding she had brought. Hands on hips and satisfied she set about unpacking the rest of her bundles; she had brought tea, bread, cheese, butter, a pie and other luxuries. "Not sure how we are going to keep these cold," she said.

"I am," Lizzy told her and pointed at the window, "Look someone has built a box onto the window sill that will do for keeping things cold for now."

So all the food items went into the box, next they set about sweeping and setting the room into some sort of semblance, eventually both sweating from exertion they stood back to admire their handiwork, the place had been transformed, there was a proper curtain hanging at the window, the bed was made, the pots and pans that Shelley had brought with her were now stashed in the dresser with the things Lizzy had found, a lacy cloth was laid on the table and a small pretty rug lay on the floor.

"It doesn't look so bad now, in fact quite homely," Shelley announced.

Lizzy hugged her friend, "Thank you, Shell, what would I do without you?" she told her.

"Well for a start get a brew on and then you can tell me what's going on," she told Lizzy. With the tea made and the pair of them sitting cross-legged on the bed Lizzy began to tell Shelley what the problem was, when she had finished Shelley took her into her arms and together they cried, gently rocking, exhausted from all the work and tears not to mention the fact that it was now the early hours both women climbed into bed, cuddled up and fell asleep.

Chapter 52

The next day when Lizzy didn't appear for breakfast Hilda went up to her room, she knocked on the door and upon not hearing anything she went in, the room was tidy and the bed made, there was a note propped up on the dressing table mirror, she opened it and began to read.

'Dear Hilda, I'm sorry I did not feel able to say goodbye, but I was scared you would stop me. I have not gone far but I feel that I need to disappear for a while, well at least until the baby is born. I don't want anyone to know I am carrying a child as it will be impossible for me to keep it under the circumstances, I will keep in touch, but please can you keep this between us, I don't want Luke or Gerry to know about the baby, if Luke gets in touch will you tell him I am well and that I have gone with Shelley to the country for a little while, I don't want him to worry. Thank you for your support over the last few months. All my love, Lizzy.'

Hilda knew in her heart that this was one of the hardest things Lizzy would have to do, to leave the comfort of those who loved and cared for her, let alone being alone with a baby growing inside her, she respected the young woman's courage, but feared for her safety, she hoped Lizzy would keep herself safe.

Chapter 53

As the weeks went by, Lizzy grew bigger and bigger she rarely left the room for fear of bumping into someone she knew, she relied heavily on Shelley's help and would be forever indebted to her friend. Shelley found her some clothes from a second hand shop and altered them accordingly as Lizzy grew bigger, the pair of them spent many a long hour in that room talking about the future and it became home for them both as Shelly spent every spare minute with her friend. Spring went and summer came, the small attic room became unbearably hot and Lizzy had no choice but to venture out for the coolness of the slums, always covering her head and never making eye contact, the good thing about the slums is that no one was interested in a lone woman walking about alone, to an outsider she looked no different to the poor women that lived there. The room was cooler at night and with the window opened as far as it could Lizzy would sit for hours relishing the coolness of the night, she would listen to the drunks coming back from the pub, the prostitutes shouting to each other and the boat horns from the docks, often she felt at peace, the baby moved and kicked within her and she would protectively place her hands upon her swollen stomach wondering what lay ahead for them both, would she be able to keep this secret? She missed Luke with a passion, the pain felt like a physical one, her heart ached for his arms around her, his lips upon hers and his gentle touch, she wondered how he was and if he missed her, too. As the weather turned and the temperature dropped Lizzy knew her time must be near, she was scared and she knew Shelley shared her fears, neither of them had any experience of childbirth, but Lizzy was confident they would be OK, after all how hard could it be? The women round here dropped them out as if they were shelling peas and carried on with their chores straight after.

Miles away much like Lizzy, Luke was sat in his room wishing he could hold her in his arms and smell her familiar scent. What was meant to be a few weeks was turning into a few months, Gerry was doing his hardest to sway the filth but it was proving harder than he had thought so sadly Luke had no choice he was stuck here while his sweetheart was in the country with Shelley. He sighed and imagined all the catching up they would be doing when they would be reunited again and frankly he couldn't wait, but at least he knew she was safe with Shelley.

Chapter 54

Like Christmas and Luke's birthday, Lizzy's birthday came and went, she did not feel much like celebrating, her heart was heavy with fear, the fear of giving birth, the anguish in the knowledge that she knew she could not keep her baby. It all felt such a mess and she felt helpless at the unfairness of the cruel blow she had been dealt.

Chapter 55

It was now September and it had been raining all day, it wasn't too cold but extremely wet, the roof had sprung a leak and Lizzy had a saucepan in the middle of the floor to catch the drips, she had felt restless all day and now she felt proper worn out so she laid on the bed and drifted into a restless sleep, she awoke with a searing pain shooting through her stomach and down between her legs, she sat up gasping, not sure what was wrong then as the sleep left her and she became alert she realised what was happening, the baby was coming.

The pain subsided and Lizzy got up. Wrapping her robe around her she went to the burner and put the kettle on to heat, her back was so painful and she had to sit in the chair as the pain made her giddy. Seconds later another pain ripped through her body, she wrapped her arms around her body and groaned through the pain, with sweat running into her eyes she gasped as it passed, breathing heavily she attempted to get up but as another pain started she fell to her knees, panting and this is how Shelley found her several minutes later. Shelley managed to get her up onto the bed and was wiping her face with a cool flannel as another pain subsided. Lizzy couldn't stay still the pain was that intense; she kept getting up, sitting down and getting up again. As more time passed she was so drained she had no energy to scream out and had begun to whimper. Shelley was worried, this didn't seem right; she helped Lizzy to her feet yet again and as she stood her waters broke all over Shelley's shoes, but there was a lot of blood and Shelley knew she had to do something.

"Liz, I'll be back in a minute," she told her,

"No!" Lizzy screamed at her "Don't leave me, please."

Shelley wiped her face and said, "I need to get help, Liz, I won't be long I promise."

She helped Lizzy back on the bed, grabbed her coat, ran down the stairs and out into the night, as she rounded the corner she found a taxi and jumped in the back, she instructed the taxi and they were on their way. To Shelley it seemed the longest journey ever, eventually they pulled up in front of the huge house, she sprinted from the car and banged on the door, Hilda came to the door followed by Gerry and Shelley had no choice but to tell Hilda she needed her and the baby was coming, she glanced at Gerry who stood dumbstruck in front of her, had he heard right, Lizzy, slum, baby?

Hilda dismissed the taxi and fetched her coat, "Gerry get the car started," she instructed him, but when he just stared at her she shouted, "GERRY CAR NOW!" he looked at both women, grabbed his coat and was out the door and in the car starting it up. Hilda and Shelley climbed in the back. "Strongway Street," she told him "We need to get Nancy; she'll know what to do."

With Gerry driving they were soon back with Nancy at the house, Shelley led the way, but as they neared the third floor they heard Lizzy screaming. Spurred on, Shelley burst into the room, Lizzy was soaked to the bone with sweat and blood was staining her nightie she was on all fours on the floor panting and moaning. Nancy took charge, issuing orders for water, towels and her bag; she knelt down next to Lizzy and quietly spoke to her.

"We need to get you back on the bed lass; I need to see what's going on." She helped Lizzy to her feet and helped her onto the bed. Gerry just stood at the door looking around at the hovel that this poor gal had been living in for the past few months. Oh he could see she had tried to make it nice, but this place was the pits, he didn't know what to think of this situation, all the while he had been telling Luke that Lizzy was fine, she was still in the country with Shelley and all along she had been holed up here, like this in a proper shithole. He saw Lizzy screaming in pain, the blood and there was enough of it. Realising he was stood there, Hilda ushered him from the room and shut the door leaving him at the top of the stairs. He looked around him at the state of the walls, the threadbare stairs and shook his head, how can people still have to live like this? Behind him he could hear Lizzy groaning and in front of him he saw filth; with a sigh he sat on the step and waited.

Chapter 56

Nancy could see the baby's head crowning but Lizzy was a wee slip of a thing and she'd not stretched enough to push it out, she knew that the baby would be in distress and she needed to get it out sooner rather than later, clearly Lizzy couldn't take much more.

Holding her hand Nancy said, "Lizzy the baby needs to come out, but it needs some help, I'm going to try forceps, OK?"

Lizzy nodded, she had never in her life experienced or expected to ever experience pain like this and frankly it was like no other, she believed she would rip in two if something didn't happen soon.

"Hilda, hold her hands," Nancy told her. "Lizzy, this is going to hurt, but I can't help that, we need to get baby out."

Lizzy nodded and Nancy carefully positioned the forceps and gently pushed from side to side to insert them, Lizzy squeezed Hilda's hand in an iron grip as the next contraction started.

"Lizzy, when you get the urge I need you to push down as hard as you can." Lizzy felt the pain rising and pushed down as hard as she could, at the same time Nancy pulled and the head was born, the release of pressure and with that some of the pain, was a god send for Lizzy, she fell back against the pillow exhausted. "Lizzy, I need one more big push when the pain starts," Nancy told her. As if on cue the pain began to rise once more and holding her breath, Lizzy pushed for all she was worth. The baby slid out but there was no noise. Nancy wrapped it in a towel and began rubbing hard suddenly the baby let out a cry and Nancy breathed a sigh of relief. She cleaned the baby's face and handed it to Lizzy. "Lizzy, it's a wee girl and beautiful she is, too."

Lizzy looked down at this tiny pink bundle and instantly felt such love for this tiny person, her baby. Nancy looked upon mother and child, she loved this part when all was well and she'd helped bring a new life into the world.

"Lizzy, we are nearly done, I need you to help me now; you need to push out the afterbirth. I know you're tired, darling, but we need to sort you out."

Lizzy also needed a couple of stitches, so Nancy handed the baby to Hilda and started sorting Lizzy out. Hilda wrapped the baby in a blanket and opened the door, Gerry was already on his feet at the door waiting, he'd heard the cry and now wanted to see the baby, as he looked down at it he felt a surge of caring for this tiny new born baby, so helpless and innocent, he looked up at Hilda and she saw tears in his eyes. Smiling to herself she knew that one day Gerry would want a child, his compassion spoke volumes.

Chapter 57

A while later with the room tidied, Lizzy washed and changed, the baby in her arms, Hilda, Gerry, Nancy and Shelley were sat around the bed enjoying a cup of tea and chatting, Gerry was the first to ask.

"Lizzy, why didn't you tell me?" then looking at Hilda. "Clearly you knew?" Lizzy reached for his hand and held it.

"I couldn't tell you and don't blame Hilda I asked her not to tell anyone, I didn't want Luke to find out or anyone really," she said.

"But why?" Gerry asked her, so she told him and when she had finished he saw her anguish and his heart broke for her.

Shortly after they rose to leave. Nancy promised she would be back later to check on them both and they left, at the top of the stairs Gerry paused and went back into the room.

"Lizzy," he said, "I won't tell anyone, your secret is safe with me," he kissed the top of her head and left.

Shelley stayed with Lizzy, they pulled out a draw and padded it out for a bed, Shelley laid the sleeping baby in it and climbed into bed with Lizzy; they chatted quietly for a few minutes and then slept.

Chapter 58

Lizzy knew that the next few days with her daughter were crucial for as much as it broke her heart she could not keep her, she spent the next two weeks with her daughter and grew to love her, she knew every inch of her and the smell of her, she wanted to embed these memories onto her heart so that she would never forget her, on the last night she sent Shelley home as she wanted to be alone with her daughter, she talked to her for hours and gave her a name. As morning dawned, Lizzy slipped from the house and sticking to the shadows she made her journey, it was a fitting morning for this end to a chapter of her life, it was cold and foggy, damp and slippery but carefully Lizzy went on. Inwardly her heart was breaking, but she believed this was the best thing she could do. How could she expect Luke to love and accept this baby not knowing who the father was? People could be so cruel and they had long memories. Her baby needed a family that would love her with no stigma attached, where no one knew what had happened. She rounded the corner and saw the lights shining, she made her way up the steps and into the warmth of the hospital, looking around she saw not a soul and gently she laid her baby down and pushed the note into her blankets. She whispered to her, kissed her tenderly and left as quietly as she had come, with her heart breaking she moved numbly through the streets, alone and distraught. Deep down she knew this was the right thing to do and this was the start of a new life for her baby, her beautiful Lucy.

WHAT WAS THAT NOISE?

What was that noise? Am I dreaming or am I awake? There it was again, no, I am definitely awake.

Ellie clung tighter to the bed covers, listening. What had roused her from her sleep? It was still dark and peeking out to look at the clock told her that it was still night time; the red digital numbers shone brightly telling her it was only 2.45 a.m. "I know I heard something," she murmured to herself. Knowing she would not be able to sleep left only one answer, "I must get up and see what that noise was," she said to the darkness, just to check nothing was amiss. Quietly she slid from beneath the warmth of the duvet and gingerly crept to the bedroom door. Just as she reached out to turn the doorknob she heard it again. Terrified now, heart beating so loudly she was sure whoever was downstairs would surely be able to hear. She looked around wildly searching for something, a weapon she could use to defend herself. Her eyes settled upon Joe's old baseball bat propped up against the wardrobe door. Creeping over to it she grasped it in her shaking hand and went back to the door. "Calm down," she told herself, "you need to do this, now get a grip!"

Mustering up some courage from the depths of God knows where she quietly opened the bedroom door and stood there listening. Nothing but the silence of darkness. Then bang, there it was again. Startled, Ellie nearly dropped the bat; her whole body was trembling with fear, fear of what or who could be making that noise. She crept along the landing and slowly edged her way down the stairs, a silent lone figure gripping the banister with one hand and the baseball bat with the other. Halfway down she took care to avoid the middle step that always creaked when stepped on.

After what seemed like the longest set of stairs ever, she reached the bottom. Peering into the darkness she willed her eyes to see, but there was nothing, just eerie darkness. She took a shaky breath and snapped on the hallway light, arm raised, bat in hand ready to defend herself. Nothing, just the familiar surroundings of her small hallway.

Moving forward to the lounge she snapped on that light, too; again, nothing out of place. Slowly the fear subsided and she started to feel silly. She next made for the kitchen; nothing wrong there either. Leaning up against the doorframe she let out a long sigh, realising she must have been holding her breath in trepidation. Feeling much braver she checked everywhere, until all the lights were blazing brightly and she was completely sure nothing was out of place in her tiny but cosy house.

"Well I may as well have a cup of tea as I am up and now wide awake," she said to herself. So, propping the baseball bat up against the door, she wandered back into the kitchen to put the kettle on and 'bang' there was the noise again! Ellie nearly died of fright there and then on the pretty pale blue lino; then she realised where the noise was coming from. Just above her line of vision was the small kitchen window hanging loosely away from its fastening and banging ominously every time the wind picked up. Laughing to herself she reached up and fastened it shut then retrieved the small key from the eggcup on the windowsill and locked the window.

She then flicked on the kettle and reached for a mug. As she stood there waiting for it to boil she thought to herself, 'I am sure I closed and locked all the windows before I went to bed…?' Then argued with herself out loud, "I must have missed this one." The kettle boiled and she poured boiling water over the teabag. The sweet fruity aromas of the herbal teabag filled her senses. Taking the mug she sat down at the table. Then she saw it, just sat there staring at the small brown package on the table, dread creeping upon her once again, cold sweat breaking out all over her body. This time she knew her mind was not overreacting or playing tricks on her; she reached a shaky, clammy hand for her phone and dialled 911.

Six months previous Ellie had been through one of the most traumatic times of her young life.

Although only 26 she had achieved a lot. She had joined the NYPD and had worked her way up through the ranks and was now one of the best homicide detectives in her department. She loved her job and devoted most of her time to her work, socialised with work colleagues and basically her job was her life. She was partnered by Shaun McNally with whom she had a great relationship in and out of the precinct. She was classed as a member of his family and felt loved and welcomed by his wife and three children. Shaun was ten years older than Ellie so naturally had taken her under his wing.

It was through Shaun she had met Joe. She remembered the first time she met him with warm delight. It had been at one of the many barbeques Shaun and Lisa had had all throughout the balmy summer evenings. He had been standing there chatting to a colleague when Ellie entered the room. Instantly their eyes made contact across the crowded room; a warm tingle spread through her as she stood there staring back at the most amazing blue eyes she had ever seen. He was around six foot, with fiery red hair, curling gently around his face line, and a body to die for: big, broad and most definitely all muscle. He began walking towards her and realising her mouth was hanging open like a dog seeing his last supper, she composed herself. He introduced himself and she breathlessly responded and raised her hand to shake his outstretched one. The minute his hand touched hers her skin tingled as if an electric charge was running through her whole being. From that day they had spent every available opportunity together. You could say they were besotted with each other, or more unfashionably that they were totally in love with one another: soul mates.

Joe worked in the local morgue and was a renowned pathologist in his own right. For both of them work was hard with many unsociable hours, but their love survived and grew. After seven months they decided to look for a small house together, each handing notice in on their flats. They found a delightful one-bedroomed house in a good neighbourhood not far from the city and made a home for themselves; life was happy and things were going well.

It was another sunny day as Ellie rose and plodded through to the bathroom to run a shower. Joe had been on an early shift and had left two hours earlier; she could still feel his gentle caresses lingering on her body as she stood under the warm jets of the shower. Closing her eyes she could see his lips half open, moving down towards her for one of those delicious kisses she loved so much about him, the stubble on his chin tickling her chin. The passion they had for one another still surprised her and the feelings he evoked within her were just as strong as they had been that very first time they had made love under the stars. She felt her body begin to tingle and her nipples harden as she drifted back to that first night. Her hand reached lower and she touched herself remembering that first orgasm he had given her, literally the earth had moved and as her body had convulsed she had never known a force so powerful. She could feel herself getting wet and this brought her back to the present: the tingling made her wish he was with her soaping her gently with the jasmine-scented body wash she loved so much.

With a sigh she washed herself and turned off the shower, making a promise to herself to seduce Joe tonight and show him how much she loved him.

The precinct was warm and had its usual high level of banter drifting across the various fans blowing out some short relief of cool air. Ellie grabbed a coffee and a doughnut and sauntered over to her desk that sat opposite Shaun's. He was nowhere to be seen, so she started checking the several messages that were on her desk. One solitary pink envelope caught her eye. Curiously she picked it up and opened it; she pulled out a piece of matching pink paper, unfolded it and began to read. The letter was written in black bold writing and was a threat not to herself but to the man she loved dearly with all her heart. As she read it a cold clammy feeling overtook her, the dread in those words slowly getting a grip upon her heart like an iron fist. She was disturbed from her panicked state by a voice from behind.

"What the hell…?" Shaun was standing over her looking at the letter in her hand. Ellie looked up at him with tear-filled eyes and just shook her head. The disbelief that someone could threaten something so horrendous was beyond her comprehension. All her years working within the 21st precinct had hardened her to most things; she had seen what she thought were the most harrowing things that life could dredge up. Shaun took the letter from her and reread it. Shaking his head he spoke to Ellie but she could not comprehend his words, the shock of what was happening or had maybe already happened completely overwhelming her. Shaun shook her to rouse her from her reverie, then suddenly she was back, alert and on her feet. The first thing she did was reach for the phone and rang Joe's personal line.

"Pick up, pick up please," she murmured, but the line just rang and rang. Shaun was on the other phone ringing the head of the mortuary. Ellie looked over at him, imploring him to have found the whereabouts of Joe. She waited, aware that the room had now gone silent, everyone's eyes focused on Shaun. When he had finished speaking he replaced the phone and looked up at her, shaking his head. Then he spoke, his words loud in the silence of the room.

"He didn't turn up for his shift this morning, Ellie, try his mobile."

Ellie groped around in her bag for her phone. She tapped in his number and waited, willing him to answer. Nothing. Helplessly, she looked up at Shaun.

"Right, let's get the ball rolling, Dan fetch Stevens." Shaun motioned to Dan, one of the other detectives, to hurry. Stevens was the Inspector in charge of the 21st precinct; he came marching in to see what was going on, closely followed by Dan.

"So what do we have here?"

Shaun started to tell Stevens what had occurred. Stevens turned to Ellie with a look of sympathy in his soft brown eyes. He had been in charge of this rowdy bunch of detectives for a long time and each one was dear to him in their own way. He picked up the letter and read it out loud:

'Ellie, the detective!!

We'll solve this, bitch.

If you want to see Joe alive then do as I say.

That last case you went too far and now I'm not playing games anymore.

You will drop the case on Angelo Sambrinni, you will not press the charges and you will let him go. If he is not released by 4 pm then Joe will be sent back to you piece by piece. And don't try to mess with me bitch, you know what I am capable of!! Do you really want more blood on your hands?

Remember you have until 4pm.

R'

Stevens looked around, everyone stood in silence, taking in what the letter had said.

"Right, Shaun, get the District Attorney on the line and tell him I want him in my office now. Ellie, who is R?"

Ellie looked up at him and suddenly she knew who and why they were doing this.

Last month she had finally closed the case she was working on; it involved a gang of Italians who thought they could play at being the mafia and were above the law. She and Shaun had taken them down one by one: there had been a lot of bloodshed and many casualties, but finally they had taken Angelo Sambrinni alive. They believed he was the ringleader of this murderous group, but there had been a niggling thought at the back of her mind since the case had been closed. It had been too easy to find and arrest Sambrinni; what if there was someone higher? She had dismissed the thought and gotten on with the other cases that had backlogged on her desk.

That niggling thought had now come back to haunt her, big style.

"Shaun, there must have been someone higher up the chain than Sambrinni, this must be R," she said.

"Who else did we miss? We covered this with a fine toothcomb!"

Stevens turned from the other detectives whom he had been giving instructions to and listened to Ellie and Shaun going over the case that had created war between the cops and this gang. It had not been an easy case; there had been too many backhanders going around and many officials had been arrested as a result of this case, but his detectives had done their jobs and gone beyond the call of duty to see to it that the culprits paid the price. He was incredibly proud of all of them.

"Firstly get that letter down to forensics and see if they can lift any prints, then, Shaun, you and Ellie see if you can trace Joe's car, backtrack his journey from home; maybe they left some evidence. Dan, when the District Attorney arrives, bring him to my office. The rest of you get thinking." With that Stevens turned and marched back to his office.

Ellie carefully put the letter into an evidence bag, grabbed her bag and followed Shaun out of the office and down to forensics.

Joe had been in an exceptionally good mood this morning as he pulled on his jacket and grabbed his car keys. He let himself out of the front door and ran down the steps, a smile lingering on his lips. Remembering the alarm going off and him reaching for Ellie, he could feel her soft warm body as it had moulded into him. Although it had been early and still dark he had felt the stirrings of an erection as her soft cheeks had begun caressing him, he had reached round and found to his delight an erect nipple straining against the silky chemise she was wearing. He pinched it gently between his thumb and forefinger and a moan escaped from Ellie's lips. Roughly he pushed her onto her back and his mouth sought hers, his tongue probing the inside of her mouth, she kissed him back with the same passion and urgency. She reached down and her hand encircled around his erection, growing harder in her delicate caress. He gasped and felt her lips smile beneath his. He lowered his head and now it was her turn to gasp as he found her erect nipple and gently suckled it into his mouth. Her back arched and she manoeuvred him over her; his fingers found her soft mass of hair and he teased, she groaned and arched her body up to meet his hand. Gently he slid two fingers inside her; he in turn gasped at finding her so wet and ready for him.

"Please," she had begged, "I want you inside of me."

Joe needed no further encouragement and he gently penetrated her, thrusting his throbbing member into her. She tightened her legs around him and pushed upwards to meet him, forcing him deeper inside her. Together as one they moved with each other; he could feel the force of his orgasm rising to fever pitch and then she came, falling apart around him as he followed, pumping harder and harder, wanting to get as far into her as he could. Her orgasm had taken them to heights that took both their breaths away, her pulsating around his member became more than he could bear and he came with a force that had his body quivering as he filled her. She gasped his name and came again.

They lay together, covered in a sheen of sweat, both spent and their hearts beating wildly. As their senses had calmed he had leant down and kissed her passionately, telling her he loved her. Then he had risen, showered, dressed and was now walking towards his jeep with a smile upon his face and a spring in his step. 'God, I love her so much,' he thought to himself and then he felt a pain in his head and his last memory was of falling.

Joe came to on a cold stone floor. He blinked several times and tried to remember what had happened, but his head hurt and everything felt fuzzy. He gingerly touched the back of his head and found an egg-sized lump. He tried to sit up but a wave of dizziness came over him and he vomited. As he retched he began to remember; he had been on the way to his jeep and then what? He tried to remember the rest but could remember nothing except he was not where he was supposed to be. He was cold and as well as a sore head, his throat hurt from retching.

"Where am I?" he said to himself; he could see nothing but pitch black. He felt around him and could feel nothing but stone. Then he heard a noise and a door opened, flooding him in light. A man stood there filling the doorway; he was huge and, boy, was he ugly!

"So, lover boy is awake then," the man drawled in a heavy Southern accent. He was carrying a tray with a steaming mug and a plate. "Here, I have brought you some tea and a sandwich; we don't want you dying on us just yet!" He grinned a toothless grin and Joe shuddered.

"Who are you, what do you want and why am I here?" Joe croaked. The man put down the tray, flicked on the light and left.

Joe heard the bolt slide across and was once again alone. He sat there looking around at his surroundings. He appeared to be in a cellar of some sort; no window, just a mattress on the floor and scurrying, which he hoped was nothing more hostile than rats! He slowly stood and the dizziness washed over him once more, but it passed and Joe went over to the tray and picked up the mug. He drank thirstily and looked around him once more. "Where the hell am I?" he said to the walls. They gave no answer. He sat on the mattress and waited, but for what he had no idea.

Ellie, Shaun, Stevens, Dan, Peter Wycliffe the District Attorney, Sam Edwards the precinct's profiler and Joe's boss, Cheryl Lambert, were all in the meeting room going over what they were to do next. Stevens started first.

"We have decided we will release Sambrinni on bail, then we will tail him and have him under surveillance. We will watch his every move if he as much as shits we will know about it!"

Each specialist gave details of what they had found out in the two hours they had each been following their own leads.

Stevens again: "So now we are done. We will let Sambrinni out at 12 midday and then see where he leads us. Dan, you and Phil (Dan's partner) are on surveillance duties and I want to know where he goes from custody because he will have to receive some word from R and as we are no nearer to finding out who R is we need to watch him like a hawk."

Ellie began to protest, "I need to follow him; he may take us to Joe."

"No, Ellie, if you are there you will be recognised. Dan and Phil were not involved in the case and are not known, they won't be recognised."

"I can't just sit here and do nothing," Ellie protested.

"I know you are feeling that you need to find this arsehole, Ellie, but please go with me on this. I promise you we will find Joe, you have my word on it; he is a good friend and we will not let anything happen to him."

Ellie looked towards Stevens and believed him. She knew he had pulled out all the stops by getting the District Attorney to release Sambrinni, knowing that there was always the chance he could make a run for it and never be seen again.

"Right we all know what we are doing so let's get to it, team, and hopefully we will end this day with Joe back and Sambrinni's boss behind bars where he belongs. Good luck all of you."

With that Stevens rose from the table and left the room. Shaun and Ellie left and resumed their seats at their desk.

Joe didn't know how long he had sat there; as there was no window he didn't know if it was day or night. He didn't know why he was there. He wondered what Ellie was doing right now; had she missed him, did she even know he was gone? *I don't want to die yet, things are going so well.* He remembered the ring he had bought two days ago and had hidden in his locker at work so Ellie wouldn't find it. He had booked a table at the infamous Deluchio's for tonight and he was going to propose to her. He loved her so much and wanted to spend the rest of his life with her, have kids, grow old with her.

He was roused from his daydreaming by the bolt on the door being pulled back; he stood, determined to get answers. The big man was back, filling the doorframe.

"C'mon, you, it's time to go."

Joe followed him through the door into a small room. The big man motioned for him to sit. He sat and waited. A door on the other side of the room opened and a man entered. He was wearing an expensively tailored suit; he was medium build and had a foreign look about him, but what caught Joe the most was the man's piercing green eyes – evil shone in them.

He took a seat opposite Joe and produced a cigar from his jacket; he trimmed the end, put it between his lips, lit it and drew on it hard; he blew the smoke out straight into Joe's face. Joe supressed a cough and held his tongue.

"Well, Joe, why do you think you are here?"

The accent was foreign to Joe and he couldn't quite place it.

"I don't know," Joe replied. "What do you want?"

The man puffed on his cigar and eyed Joe with those evil eyes, a touch of laughter playing around the corners.

"Ellie," the man said.

Joe jumped up, only to be shoved back down. "What have you done to her?" he asked.

"Nothing, yet," the man said with menace. "It's what she can do for you. How much do you think she loves you, eh, Joe? Enough to help me with my little problem or will she leave you here to rot?"

"What has this got to do with Ellie and who the hell are you?" Joe spat at the man, his fists clenched in his lap.

The man eyed him slowly, rolling his cigar around his mouth, "My name is Ricardo Sambrinni, and I want something from your girlfriend. She has until 4 p.m. to follow my wishes and if she doesn't then we will be sending you back to her in pieces."

Joe just stared at this vulgar little man: where did he know that name from? Then it hit him, of course Sambrinni – that was the case Ellie and Shaun had been working on for the past five months. They had arrested a guy named Angelo, the ringleader and boss. He was now locked up and awaiting trial for murder, rape, blackmail, prostitution, and extortion.

Ricardo looked at his expensive Rolex and eyed Joe. "By my estimation she now has five hours to seal your fate," he said and rose. "If you see me back then you know she has abandoned you and that you will be dead!" Joe lost his temper and flew at him, but he was restrained and punched by the big guy with no teeth, who shoved him back in the chair. Joe sat there, winded and gripping his chest; he was sure he had sustained at least a couple of broken ribs.

"Fuck you," he spat at Ricardo through clenched teeth. This earned him a punch to the jaw.

"Show some respect for the boss, man," the hired thug spat back at Joe. On that note he was dragged from the chair and thrown back into the cellar; the door clanked shut behind him and the bolt shot across.

Joe lay on the floor stunned by the words he had just heard. "Oh, Ellie, I'm so sorry I have put you in this position." His mind wandered back to the last time he had seen her, curled up in their bed, relaxed, a soft smile on her lips, satiated from their love making. Tears filled his eyes and he knew any chance of escape was hopeless; he could only wait, pray and hope for a small miracle.

Dan and Phil followed the cab Angelo had jumped in after being released on bail. He had led to them to a hotel called the Hotel Medici; it was a nice, middle-class place with a valet on the door. They had parked up and were watching the front door. As they sat waiting for Angelo to make an appearance, Dan spotted Shaun's car pull in a few cars down.

He dialled Ellie's phone and when she picked up he asked, "What took you so long, guys?"

"Very funny, Dan," she retorted. They all sat waiting for an hour or so. Shaun let out a long sigh.

"Stevens is gonna have our arses for this!"

Ellie looked over at him and also sighed, "You can always go, Shaun, I don't want you to get into trouble, too, but I can't just sit around waiting for something to happen. We are not doing any harm just watching."

Shaun looked across at his partner: a hard person as far as the job was concerned, but she had feelings when it came to the people she loved. He loved this woman like a sister and he felt for her. He reached out and grasped her hand.

"We will find this son of a bitch, Ellie."

She looked back at him and felt the tears fall; she felt so useless. Was Joe OK? Was he hurt or was he even still alive? These men were ruthless and didn't care who they hurt in the process of getting what they wanted. So, they sat there and watched and waited. An hour or so had passed when a black SUV pulled up to the kerb at the Hotel Medici. Angelo ran down the steps and jumped in the front; it screeched off, followed by Dan and Phil keeping a couple of cars back so as not to get spotted and rumbled for following. Ellie and Shaun were also tailing the SUV. It drove around for about half an hour, going nowhere in particular. "Checking there's no tail I bet," said Shaun. The radio crackled and Phil's voice came over the radio.

"I know you two are there behind us, any idea where this loser is headed?"

Ellie picked up the radio and replied, "No idea, Phil, Shaun thinks they are making sure they don't have a tail,"

"Yep, maybe you're right," Phil replied.

After a few more minutes the SUV came to a stop outside an old-fashioned townhouse in the slum district. Angelo got out and looked around him. The two plain police cars had also stopped, all the occupants watching. Ellie had already taken out her firearm and was checking it was loaded and cocked ready to go. Shaun picked up the radio and radioed headquarters. Down the line came Stevens's voice.

"I knew you both would be there, do you ever obey orders, you two?"

"Sorry, sir," came Ellie's voice. "It's all my fault, I made Shaun come and Phil and Dan cover for me, I couldn't just sit around and wait!" She heard Stevens let out a long sigh.

"Look, Ellie, I would not have expected any less of you and there was no way your colleagues would have let you do it alone or ratted on you. All I will say to you all, is nail that bastard once and for all!"

"Yes, sir," they all chorused.

They got out of their cars and came together at the end of the street, hidden away from the townhouse.

"How are we going to do this?" asked Phil. Shaun spoke up and voiced his idea to his fellow officers. Once they were all sure they knew what each was doing they set out, each alone to carry out their tasks. Back up was on its way so they were not totally alone. Shaun and Ellie took the back; they crept up the wooden steps onto the dilapidated veranda and listened – no sound could be heard from within. Shaun quietly tried the rickety back door, amazed when it opened; he beckoned to Ellie to cover him.

Together they entered what seemed to be a laundry room. There was an old rusted washing machine and rags littered the floor. Silently they carried on through to a spacious dining area. They paused, listening; they could hear the faint hum of voices coming from the next room. A chair scraped across the floor followed by a thud. Shaun and Ellie made their way across the room and headed to the only door that appeared to be in the musty room. They leaned against it and listened again: the voices were louder and they could make out some words.

"Where is the bastard? Bring him out here. If I can't have that bitch at least I can take what she loves, bring him out now!" Angelo's words ripped through Ellie's heart, she stepped forward but Shaun held her still.

No, he mouthed, vigorously shaking his head. Another door opened and they could hear dragging, then an older voice commanding someone to sit, there was a scuffle and Angelo's voice drifted through the door again.

"What's it feel like, eh? To be held against your will, your bitch did that to me and I'm going to rip you apart limb by limb, you ginger bastard!"

Ellie looked at Shaun with a look of sheer desperation, pleading with him to let her help, again he shook his head and mouthed, *We need to wait, hang in there*.

Joe spoke, "You deserved everything you had coming to you, how long did you think you could carry on the way you were without getting caught? Regardless of what you do to me, Ellie will hunt you down; mark my words, of that you can be sure."

"She will never find me, or you, by the time I have finished with you!" said Angelo. Then a different voice was heard, older calmer.

"Son, calm down, they will never trace us, there is no need for more blood to be shed, we will just leave him locked up in the cellar, it will be months before anyone finds him and by then he will have gone mad locked up on his own, with no food and water he won't last long." Then followed an argument between father and son, in the end Angelo relented. "OK, but just one go, let me scar that pretty face of his as a reminder of me while he is locked up alone."

Horrified Ellie turned to Shaun; *We must do it now*, her eyes pleaded at him. As if the others knew the radio clicked once – the signal from Phil to say they were in position. With that, Ellie needed no second signal she shoved her shoulder against the door, gun raised and fell into the room, regaining her balance, Phil had come through the front and Shaun was hot on her heels. "Freeze, police," she yelled, she took in the room: Joe slumped in a chair barely conscious; Angelo; a big giant of a man; and an older man with a similar look to Angelo. Everyone stood stock still for a second then Angelo drew a gun and was behind Joe with the barrel rammed against his forehead, safety off, daring Ellie to come closer, just to give him the excuse.

Ellie took in the three men and looked around her – where was Dan? Just as the thought crossed her mind, a shot rang out and Angelo crumpled to the floor, a bullet hole between his eyes, eyes that stared vacantly, the look of a dead man. All hell broke loose, the older man went down on his knees at his son's side, Shaun handcuffed the big man, and Phil went over to the older man, cuffed him and dragged him away from Angelo's prone body. Ellie crouched by Joe and gently lifted his head, his eyes flickered open and he looked at her, recognition shining in his tear-filled eyes.

"You came for me?" he whispered.

"Of course I came for you, Joe, you are my life. I love you." He fell from the chair into her arms and they just sat there crying, holding each other, together.

The silence was shattered by Angelo's father screaming at Ellie, his face twisted with hatred as he spat out, "I am Ricardo: I will avenge my son's death, you will die, bitch, if it's the last thing I do!" Shaun shoved him away and shouted for back up to take the men away.

Ellie had taken Joe to the local hospital and he had been checked over. He was battered, bruised and very dehydrated but apart from that was in good shape. At around 10 p.m. they finally arrived home, Ellie ran Joe a bath and left him soaking, she went downstairs to rustle up something to eat; 20 minutes later Joe came down stairs dressed in just a pair of jeans and joined her in the kitchen. She had just dished up some pasta and he proceeded to open a bottle of Chianti. He poured them both a glass and handed her one.

They sat at the kitchen table and started to eat. Joe looked across at Ellie and she looked up meeting his gaze.

"I booked a table at Deluchio's for us tonight," he said.

"Really, what was the occasion?" Ellie asked him. He came round the table and bent down on one knee before her.

"Will you marry me, darling?" he asked her as he gently grasped her hand.

Ellie's eyes widened and the love for this man swamped her. "Yes," she said breathlessly. "Yes, yes!"

He pulled her up and hugged her to him, "That was why I booked the table. I wanted to do this properly, but now seems a good a time as any. I have a ring, but I hid it in my locker at work so you will have to wait for a ring."

Ellie felt the tears glistening at the back of her eyes, unable to hold on they coursed down her cheeks, "Why so sad, my darling?" Joe asked her as he kissed away the salty tears.

"I thought I had lost you forever," she stammered, "I couldn't bear that, Joe, I was so scared."

He kissed her passionately, he kissed her lips, her pert little nose and her cheeks; the kisses became more urgent, he lifted her into his arms and carried her up to their bedroom. Gently he laid her on the bed and slowly undressed her, their breaths becoming raspier as their need for each other heightened. He lay down next to her naked body and caressed each part of it. She arched up to him, her body hot against his bare chest and found his mouth, their kisses filled with the urgency of two people who thought they had lost each other. They became lost in each other, touching and exploring the parts they knew best. Ellie undid the button of his jeans, lowered the zip and curled her hand around his erection, he dipped his head and kissed her every intimate part, pushing his jeans down at the same time. They lay there together naked, touching each other.

"Make love to me," she whispered, hoarsely. Joe didn't need asking twice. He rolled on top of her and gently pushed his erection inside her, moving in and out with practised slowness, just touching her with the tip of his member as he withdrew, only to plunge back into her soft wetness with a force that made her gasp. She gripped his shoulders, rising up to meet him; kissing his chest and neck, she nuzzled his ear and whispered, "Come with me, darling."

Joe needed no more prompting, his orgasm rumbled through him like a volcanic eruption, he stiffened and gripped her tightly as he came with such force just as Ellie's orgasm erupted around him, she held him tightly as the final spasms of their orgasms shuddered through them both. Panting they lay in each other's arms, finally succumbing into a restful sleep.

The next few weeks flew by, what with both of them having huge workloads, but they always ate together in the evening and made time for each other whereas before the incident they may have taken each other a little for granted.

Friday the 23rd October Joe had met her from work and they walked to her car, they drove home, the weather had turned colder and it was dark but the air was fresh and crisp. They arrived home and decided on a take away, Ellie opened a bottle of Chardonnay and they chatted about their day.

"I have to go on a two-day conference on Monday; will you be okay here alone?"

"Of course," she scoffed. "I'm a police detective with a big gun! But I will miss you," she said and leaned across to kiss him. They ate their food and decided on an early night.

The alarm roused them both from their sleep. Ellie yawned and reached over Joe to switch it off; his arms came around her and he held her in his strong arms, gently kissing her neck.

"C'mon," she said returning his kisses with a firm one to his lips. "We will be late if we stay here, as nice as it would be and besides, stud, didn't you have your fill last night?"

"I could never have enough of you," he teased, tweaking her nipple. They showered, taking longer than normal as Joe decided to join her in the shower and kept her in there longer than necessary!

Ellie arrived at the precinct by 8 a.m., having kissed Joe goodbye with the promise that he would ring her from the hotel tonight. Her day passed pretty quickly. She and Shaun were working on a case of a missing family man, and they had no leads and even less to go on. Ellie arrived home around 6 p.m. She went upstairs and changed into joggers and one of Joe's T-shirts; she made herself some pasta with cream and mushrooms and opened a bottle of wine. She had just finished washing the dishes when the phone rang, it was Joe, they talked for a while, said their goodbyes and she put the phone down. Yawning, Ellie decided she would grab an early night, she locked all the windows and the doors, assured everything was safe and secure she went off up to bed, unaware that not all was as it seemed.

Having dialled 911 Ellie, went to the safe they had installed and retrieved her gun, she loaded it and then rang Shaun. He answered after two rings.

"Ellie, what's up?"

"Shaun," she said; he could hear the fear in her voice. "Someone has been in the house." She paused, listened, thinking she had heard something. Satisfied it was the wind she again spoke: "I was woken by a noise and got up to investigate, the kitchen window was unlocked and banging, I secured it, made a cuppa and then saw it!" Shaun was awake now and dragging on his jeans with one hand while still holding the phone in the other.

"Saw what, honey?"

Ellie took a deep breath and spoke again, "There is a brown package on the table, Shaun, just like the ones Angelo Sambrinni used to leave his victims."

Shaun was on his way to the door and told her, "Don't move, don't open the door to anyone, I'm on my way, be there in 15." With that he hung up.

Ellie sat there and stared at the package.

A knock at the door startled Ellie and she realised she had just been sat there staring at the package, firearm in hand ready. She rose and went to the door. "Who is there?" she asked.

"It's me, Shaun."

She opened the door and let him in. Once inside he told her there was a patrol car outside keeping watch and another was searching the area for anyone suspicious.

"Joe still away?" Shaun asked, Ellie nodded and motioned for him to come into the kitchen.

"Coffee?" she asked.

"Yes, strong please. Tell me what happened," Shaun asked as he took a seat at the table.

Ellie went over the facts and brought his coffee over to the table. "And then I rang you," she finished.

Shaun pulled a pair of latex gloves from his pocket and picked up the package, he examined it and looked up at Ellie. "You want me to open it?" he asked her. "Maybe it's not what we think, it could be some nutcase just trying to scare you, we work with enough of them!"

Ellie eyed the package and then looked back at Shaun, "Okay, let's see what's inside."

Shaun carefully unwrapped the package, to find a box. Ellie's heart was thudding as he opened the box. By the look on Shaun's face she knew what was inside: the same tell-tale scarlet lipstick. When they had been hunting the murderer of eight women, all the women had been found with this lipstick smeared around their mouths and the lipstick was found on the table next to the same brown package. This hunt had led them to Angelo Sambrinni and during their investigation they had unearthed all the other crimes he had committed, as well as getting his kicks from raping and murdering young women.

"Right, for a start we need to send this to the lab to see if they can lift any prints or any other evidence, then you need to ring Joe and check he is okay. Ellie, are you listening to me?" Shaun's voice had risen as it became clear Ellie was just staring at him vacantly. "C'mon, honey, don't fall apart on me now." He gently touched her hand. His touch brought her back to reality.

"Shaun, this is impossible, Angelo is dead, we saw Dan blow his brains out!"

Shaun sighed and replied, "I know and he was cremated so there's no way that creep has risen from the dead! I'll get this to the lab and then I'll come back around 6.30 a.m. and pick you up; I don't want you going anywhere alone. In the meantime, you call Joe and fill him in. Don't open the door for anyone but me, OK?"

"I won't," she agreed, and with that Shaun left.

Ellie reached for her phone and rang the hotel Joe was staying at, the receptionist transferred her call to his room, he picked up after three rings.

"Yeah, what time is it?" he mumbled sleepily.

"Joe, it's me," Ellie said in a shaky voice.

"Ellie, what's wrong" Joe's tone appeared panicky.

"I'm fine," she replied. "We've had a break in; I need you to come home."

She could hear rustling as he sat up, wide awake now. "I'll be home later this morning, darling. Please don't worry, we will sort it out."

They spoke for a few more minutes then she hung up, wondering if she should have told him about the package. *No, he would only worry more. I'll tell him when he gets home.* She looked at the clock, 5 a.m.; she rose and headed upstairs for the shower.

Ellie turned on the shower and waited for the water to run hot, she perched on the edge of the bath looking around the bathroom; she loved this room, with its creams and beiges, the marbled surfaces, not to mention the plush thick pile carpet. When they had bought the house she and Joe had the original bathroom completely gutted and now they had a beautiful ornate, oval-shaped tub, matching sink and toilet, but the best thing she liked was the corner walk-in shower they had fitted, just big enough for two. A smile played at the corners of her mouth as she remembered some of the wonderful times she and Joe had shared, ensconced within the glass unit!

The bathroom was filling up with steam; Ellie went back to the bedroom, placed her gun on the bedside table, took off her robe and grabbed a towel. The water was hot but soothing. She scrubbed herself all over with the jasmine body wash she always favoured, then, eyes closed, she stood, allowing the suds to wash away from her, trying not to panic too much about the package; maybe Shaun was right. Ellie switched off the shower and groped around for the towel. Instead of finding the softness of towelling, her hand brushed over something rough; her eyes flew open and there in her bathroom was a man. She tried to scream but he was quicker: his hand shot out and grabbed her, he pulled her to him and covered her mouth with his other hand. For a second she was stunned, then she began to kick and buck, trying to loosen his grip all the while being conscious of the fact she was naked.

He dragged her back to the bedroom and threw her on the bed. This knocked the wind out of her and as she tried to catch her breath he yanked her ankles and tied them with rope. Next, he bound her wrists, finally taping her mouth. Ellie lay there, unable to cover her nakedness, completely helpless. She felt the sob rising in her throat and swallowed it down, refusing to give this man the satisfaction. The man stared at her, evil green eyes roving over her body. She gasped; she had seen that look before, the evilness in those eyes. No, it was not possible, he was dead: she had seen him die with her own eyes. The man continued to stare then he spoke. His accent was heavy but not American.

"Do you know who I am, bitch?" Ellie shook her head, she knew who he looked like, but it couldn't be him. He straddled her and from his jacket produced a small knife. He traced the point down her neck, pushing hard enough to break the skin; she could feel the warmth as blood trickled down her skin. A leering smile on his lips, he flicked his tongue around them, enjoying her discomfort; she could feel him growing hard against her taut belly. *Please God, no;* her eyes filled with tears and she was unable to prevent them flowing over her lids and coursing down her cheeks. He seemed to enjoy this more, his breathing becoming laboured. Then he raised his hand and ripped off the tape. It left a burning sensation around her mouth.

"Make a noise and I'll slash that pretty face of yours," he threatened. "You figured out who I am, bitch?" he spat at her. Ellie shook her head. "Well, let me tell you a story, I had a brother, maybe you've heard of him? His name was Angelo! We were twins and because of you he was murdered in front of our father. Now it's time for you to pay the price!" Ellie stared up at him, eyes wide: how could they have not known this? "Did you like my present?"

From his pocket he brought out a lipstick. As he brought it down to her mouth she jerked her head from side to side. The blow caught her on the left side of her face. The pain shot through her and for a moment she was dazed, her mind trying to will herself from this situation: *this was not happening to her.*

Shaun went straight to the precinct, bagged the package then delivered it to forensics to be tested. He went back up to his desk and reached for the phone, he rang Stevens and filled him in on what had happened then he grabbed his jacket and made his way down to the parking lot. As he drove back to Ellie's house he mulled the night's events over in his head, "Who the hell is doing this?" he asked himself out loud. As he turned into Ellie's street he could see the patrol car parked outside; he drove up to it and wound down his window.

"Any sign of movement?" he asked.

"No, all quiet," the patrolman replied.

Shaun parked up and walked up to the front door; he gently knocked and waited. No answer, so he knocked again; still no answer. He had a strange feeling in his gut; he tried the door: locked. Where the hell was she? He walked around the house to the back and saw the door open just slightly. That gnawing feeling in his gut erupted and he drew his gun. Quietly he pushed open the door, checked the kitchen: no one there. He stood in the semi darkness and listened. The house was silent, then he heard a dull thud. He crept forward and came to the bottom of the stairs, and strained his ears, listening. He heard a low voice, but couldn't work out what was being said. It couldn't be Joe, it would take him at least five hours to drive back. Shaun began climbing the stairs; halfway up the step creaked under his weight and he cursed under his breath.

Ellie heard the stair creak; had the man? He appeared not to have.

"If you go now, no one will know you were even here," she said to him quietly.

He looked at her. "Do you think I'm stupid, bitch?" he sneered at her. "By the time I've finished with you and gone no one will know I have been here anyway. And I'm not leaving until my brother's death has been avenged!"

He roughly grabbed her breast and with the knife he traced the outline of her nipple, digging the blade in and again drawing blood. Ellie winced with the pain, then, by some miracle, over the man's shoulder she saw Shaun appear. He put his finger to his lips to motion to her not to move or speak. He raised his gun and pulled the trigger; the man fell sideways on to the bed, the knife falling from his grasp, blood seeping from the wound on the right side of his temple.

His eyes were open but unseeing; the bullet had mushed his brain and killed him outright. Ellie rolled to her side away from him, huge sobs wracking her body; she curled up. Shaun came over, picked up the knife and cut the ropes from her ankles and wrists. He then grabbed her robe and pulling her towards him he wrapped it around her, holding her gently as she sobbed. There was a crash downstairs as the patrolman broke down the door, having heard the shot. Shaun shouted down to him, "Get back up, an ambulance and the pathologist up here now." He looked down at Ellie and asked her, "Are you badly hurt? Did he…?" She looked up at him with tears in her eyes and shook her head.

The next few hours seemed a blur to Ellie. The appropriate people came and did their jobs, then she was taken to hospital and checked over. Just as she was being discharged there was a commotion outside her cubicle and a breathless Joe came round the curtain. He dropped to his knees in front of her and grabbed her hands.

"Are you hurt?" he choked out.

"I'm okay," she replied, her eyes welling with tears. She grabbed him and they held each other. The doctor and nurse left, giving them privacy.

Ellie never went back to that house; she couldn't bring herself to go. They stayed at a safe house, kindly given to them for as long as they needed, though Ellie knew this was down to Stevens's intervention. The house was put on the market and eventually sold; they bought an apartment in an upcoming block nearer to the city with a fantastic, impenetrable security system. Life slowly returned to normality, although Ellie occasionally had nightmares. She returned back to work; the bond between her and Shaun had been strong before her attack, but now it was a bond that could never be broken. He had saved her life and for that she would be eternally grateful.